CARNAGE IN A PEAR TREE

DAKOTA CASSIDY

COPYRIGHT

ACKNOWLEDGEMENTS

Cover artist: Katie Woods
Editor: Kelli Collins

Welcome to Marshmallow Hollow Mysteries! Set in the wintery seaside (and totally fictional) town of Marshmallow Hollow, Maine, where it's all Christmas all the time, and murder is hung by the chimney with care! I'm so excited to introduce you to Halliday Valentine (Hal for short), Atticus Finch—her crusty hummingbird familiar—her small gang of crime solvers, and the quirky folks from her beloved hometown.

Please note, this series is a bit of a spinoff of my Witchless in Seattle series, in that Hal and part of the gang were introduced in book 10 of the series, titled *Witch It Real Good*. But there's no need to read the Witchless series if you haven't.

That said, this is an ongoing series (not a stand-alone) and there might be some underlying mysteries that may linger from book to book, but I promise to wrap up the central mystery with a big, fat bow by each book's end! Though, please keep in mind, *Carnage in a Pear Tree* picks up right where *One Corpse Open Slay* left off.

Also note, I'm taking artistic license with places and names of things in the beautiful state of Maine—thus, any and all mistakes are mine and certainly not meant to offend.

Lastly, Christmas is my absolute favorite time of the year. I love everything about it, the decorations, the music, the gathering of friends and family, and most of all, the hope the season brings.

I hope you all love Hal, her friends, and her tiny little Christmas town as much as I do!

Dakota XXOO

CHAPTER 1

"A witch."

Uh-oh, all that wonder and awe in his voice was gone, replaced by the reality of the situation. His girlfriend was a witch.

I nodded and winced at Hobbs's flat tone. "Live and in person."

He inhaled and let out a slow breath. "Lemme say this from jump so you'll understand where I'm coming from. I'm curious by nature already, but you've just confessed something incredible—almost unbelievable. Not only that, but it's a revelation average guys like me only see in movies or on TV, so I don't know what's ridiculous of me to ask or not, okay? All I know about witches is what I've heard or read…or whatever."

"Right…" I answered slowly, unsure where he was going with this.

"That said, I'm probably gonna ask some stupid questions along the way."

Smiling, I nodded. "No questions are stupid, Hobbs," I assured, turning to face him as I tucked the blanket around us and smiled as warmly as my face would allow.

I'd just broken the news about how I'd solved a crime with my magic, and to say the information was jarring, if not fantastical to a human, was to say the Civil War was a petty squabble.

Squaring his shoulders, Hobbs finally asked, "Okay. You ready?"

"Like a roast turkey whose timer's popped."

As Christmas music played softly in the background, I watched him internally wrestle with himself before he asked, "Do you ride a broom?"

I giggled. "Okay, some questions *are* stupid."

Hobbs winced. "I did make a disclaimer."

I grinned. "And I'm only kidding. Go on. Ask away."

"*Do you ride a broom?*" he repeated in his light Southern lilt.

I gave him a blank stare. "Oh. You were serious." Shaking my head, I answered, "No. No broom."

Now it was his turn to stare blankly at me.

"Hobbs?"

He cocked his head. "Everything I was gonna ask you just flew right out of my noggin. Yet, I have a million questions."

I hesitated only a moment before I decided to rip off the rest of the Band-Aid. If I was going to get this out in the open, I might as well go all the way.

Stroking my newly adopted kitten Barbra's tiny

head as she purred contentedly in my lap, I didn't bother to temper my words.

"While you think of them, there's more you should know."

The only reaction he had was the lift of one eyebrow. "Do I need more alcohol for the 'more' part?"

"Maybe."

"I'll get some wine—"

"No need," I murmured, snapping my fingers. A bottle of Hobbs's favorite red appeared, cork already removed, with two glasses.

I figured I might need a drink, too.

To his credit, he managed to remain mostly still. Well, except for the clench of his jaw. He poured two glasses and handed one to me before he gulped his until it was gone.

Rolling his head to ease his obvious tension, he slapped his thighs as though he were mentally preparing to have a tooth pulled without anesthesia. "Okay, I'm ready. What's the more?"

"Atticus."

His strong bearded jaw shifted, but only a little. It was his eyes that gave him away this time. They went a little glassy and faraway. "Your hummingbird?"

"My hummingbird *familiar*. You know, like my guide—"

He held up a hand to stop my explanation. "I know what a familiar is."

My eyes went wide. "Do you then? How do you know about familiars?"

He shrugged and looked over my shoulder at the Christmas tree. "I know stuff, too. I'm not just some dumb cowboy from Texas. I lived in Boston for a while, you know."

I fought a smile. "Well, big city boy, bet you didn't know he talks…"

Now he made a face, as though I'd really gone too far. He sat back with a chuckle and took a gulp of his wine. "Oh, c'mon. He does not."

"Does too."

"Listen, Detective Lacey, I can buy… Wait. I *do* buy the witch thing because of that ball of light and the wine you produced out of thin air, but a talking hummingbird? Mmm, no. I didn't just fall off the chicken truck."

"I thought it was the turnip truck?"

"Where I come from, it's chickens."

"Okay, Texas, if you say so, but I'm telling the truth and I can prove it."

Now he shook his dark head, very clearly and quite firmly in the negative. "Nope. Not buyin' it."

"But I do talk, Digby Dainty, and if you intend to court my beloved little poppet of a witch, you shall make the appropriate adjustments," Atti said as he flew into the living room and hovered by the Christmas tree, his wings fluttering at lightning speed.

Now Hobbs jumped up and looked around, clear suspicion in his eyes. "That was Stiles, wasn't it? Stiles? Come on out, bud. Joke's over, but spot-on British accent. Well done."

Atticus flew right into Hobbs's direct line of vision, flapping his wings furiously. "I assure you, I'm no joke and this is no fake accent."

I saw the muscles in Hobbs's legs flex beneath his jeans as he reached behind him and felt around until his hand touched the couch, then he plopped back down, grabbing for the wine to pour more.

I rubbed his muscled arm and smiled in sympathy. "You okay?"

He gulped another half glass of wine before he said, "No. Yes. I'm not sure. But I think mostly yes." Then he shook off whatever was troubling him and said with more conviction, "*Yes.* Yes, I'm okay."

"Well, there's something to be said for the good ol' boys from Texas, isn't there? If nothing else, they give good face," Atticus muttered with his usual dry sarcasm.

"Oh, Atti," I chided. "Shush. We just told him witches are real and that you can talk. Let the man process. Don't be a toad about it."

But Hobbs held up his hand. "No, no. He's right. If I'm going to *court* you, there are adjustments to be made. Apparently, one is a talking bird."

"*Hummingbird*, fine sir," Atti corrected.

"Hummingbird," Hobbs acknowledged. "My apologies. No offense meant. Anyway, if courting you means you can produce bottles of wine out of thin air, who am I to complain?"

Atti buzzed to situate himself in front of Hobbs's face, his wings racing. "No. She absolutely will not use her magic with such careless abandon. We live amongst humans; we must behave as such in order to coexist properly. Thus, any and all alcoholic beverages or otherwise will be purchased at the liquor store."

I sighed, scooping up Barbra to nuzzle her against my cheek. "What Atti means is, I'm not supposed to use my magic unless absolutely necessary because if I get too used to doing things with a little abracadabra, I might slip and get caught. Also, we're not allowed to use our magic for personal gain. So forget that horse ranch in Spain."

Hobbs just stared at Atti.

"Hobbs?" I gave him a nudge.

He shook his head as though he'd been lost in thought. "Sorry, but this takes some getting used to. I mean Atticus, um, talking." Then he reverted his gaze back to me. "So you were saying you can't whip up a Maserati, right?"

I smiled and nodded. "Right. Nothing for personal gain."

"But you wouldn't be personally gaining, I would."

"Ahem!" Atti loudly cleared his throat. "Familiar still here. There will be no Maseratis. There won't be so much as a Big Wheel, thank you very much."

Now Hobbs laughed and held up his hands in surrender. "Okay, okay. I was just joking, Atticus. I promise not to take Hal down the path of the wicked for my own personal gain. No Big Wheels for the mere mortal." There was a moment of silence where Atticus, in his typical stoicism, didn't laugh at his joke, before

Hobbs gave me a sheepish look. "Now that we've gotten that out of the way, we're good, right?"

I wasn't sure if he was asking out of hope or terror. "Hold that thought."

Hobbs lifted his chin as Atti landed on my shoulder to lean into my ear, his deep voice tickling my eardrums. "Surely you're not going to, are you, Halliday?"

I knew exactly what he meant. "Of course I am, Atti. I have to tell him everything."

Hobbs sat quietly as the fire crackled and Stephen King, my favorite bulldog, stretched and yawned from his bed beside the flames.

This wasn't going to be fun. To find out that all this time he'd been snuggling up to my reincarnated *grandmother* out in the barn might change the dynamic of not just our relationship, but theirs.

Nana Karen loved, loved, loved Hobbs, and he loved her. He gave her carrots all the time—which as you know, she hates, but she accepts them because they're from *Hot Sauce Hobbs*, as she calls him. They'd developed a relationship, and to find out she'd been deceiving him all this time could feel like a real betrayal.

Add in that she was reincarnated in a reindeer's body, and this might just be the tipping point for my new boyfriend.

Out of the blue, Hobbs laughed as though he'd realized something. "It's Karen, right? Is she a weredeer?"

Was that a random observation or did he think all

my animals talked? But then, I guess most of mine did, didn't they?

Still, I blinked, dumbfounded. "A weredeer? What the feck's a weredeer?"

"You and Stiles read paranormal romance novels, right?" When I nodded, he said, "Then y'all know what I mean. Like a werewolf, but not? A hybrid shifter."

Suddenly, it hit me—out of all the paranormal romances Stiles and I read, some had shifters—some even had more eclectic shifters like werebeavers. Not my preferred reading, mind you (I'm a vampire-werewolf hybrid girl, myself), but I knew what Hobbs meant.

What I wanted to know was how *Hobbs* knew about them.

But then, Stiles loved a good, steamy romance novel, especially a paranormal romance, and I was being sexist for thinking men didn't read them.

Then I wondered, if Hobbs *did* read them, why he'd never mentioned it during the many book swaps Stiles and I had right under his nose.

How else would he know about hybrids and weredeer?

Anyway, I understood what he was getting at about my nana. "Ah, I get it! You mean vampires and demons and stuff, right?"

He nodded with a smile. "Yep."

"Um, nope. Karen isn't a...uh, weredeer."

"Phil? Is Phil a werecat?" His sultry Southern accent grew thicker and his eyes grew more hesitant.

I patted him on the knee and smiled to reassure him. "No. Phil's just Phil. An ornery, only-wants-to-be-loved-when-he-wants-to-be-loved mongrel of a whole cat, but all cat. Now, Karen…?"

I heard Hobbs fight a gasp and then he poured more wine, taking a long swig. "Go ahead. I'm ready."

Sighing, knowing this could break him, I gave him a guilty look, but I knew I had to say it or I'd chicken out. "Karen is my nana Karen—reincarnated…as a reindeer…"

He stared at me long and hard before he said, "So all this time I've known her, she…?"

"Yes."

"She can…"

"Talk? Yes."

"So when we were investigating…"

"The murder she was indirectly involved in?"

If you'll recall, earlier this month, nana was hauled off to the animal pokey and we thought she'd witnessed a murder. She didn't see a thing. But now I'm sure Hobbs was wondering if she really had, and if we'd talked about it.

Hobbs nodded. "Yes."

"No. She didn't see anything, but she was in the vicinity."

He swallowed hard, his Adam's apple bobbing along his tan neck as he clung to the wine glass. "And all the carrots I feed her every day?"

I grinned. "She hates those, by the way, but she really likes you, so she takes one for the team."

Now he looked downright uncomfortable. "Has she told you..."

"Told me what?"

He pulled himself to the end of the couch and set his glass down. "Never mind. Listen, I have an early meeting tomorrow. Can we finish our talk later in the afternoon? Will you be okay?"

"I'll be fine," I responded stiffly, unsure why he appeared so uncomfortable all of a sudden.

Hobbs leaned down, tipped my chin up, and gently kissed my lips. "I promise we'll talk more tomorrow, Hal. I meant what I said earlier, I just didn't realize how late it was."

"Okay," I murmured, my heart tight in my chest as he grabbed his jacket and called to Stephen King, who reluctantly waddled toward him with a yawn.

"I'll see you tomorrow, Hal," he called over his shoulder and then he was gone, the door shutting so quietly, the bells on it hardly jangled.

"Bye," I whispered...and I rather thought it really *was* goodbye.

"Halliday?" Atti said, nudging my ear.

I gulped to keep tears from falling from my eyes, my throat tight and stiff. I really thought Hobbs was going to be the one. I really, truly did. "Yes?"

"Don't project. He said he'd speak with you tomorrow. Hobbs is, if nothing else, a man of his word. If he said he'll speak with you tomorrow, he'll speak with you tomorrow."

Scooping up Barbra, I nodded, scrunching my eyes

to thwart tears. "I'm sure he will. I'm going to bed. It's been a long night."

"Halliday…" I heard the warning tone Atti took, and I knew he meant well, but I didn't want to be reminded of Hobbs's words. I was reading his body language—and his body language said this was all too much.

I was too much.

A crazy witch, her talking hummingbird familiar, and her reincarnated grandmother were just too much for Hobbs Dainty.

And that was really too bad, wasn't it?

I am what I am.

Period.

CHAPTER 2

"You ou wanna talk about it, young lady?" Nana Karen asked as I mucked her stall, the cold, early-morning air invigorating me, jolting me awake after a fitful night's sleep.

I hadn't heard a peep from Hobbs, not even a text, leaving me anxious and maybe a little angry.

"I don't."

"Aw, c'mon, Hallie-Oop. Tell your nana what's wrong. I can't bake you cookies anymore to make it better, but I sure can listen. Got the big ears to prove it," she joked, rearing back and shaking her antlers at me.

I wasn't ready to talk about last night. Hobbs had hurt my feelings, and I was still in the process of chalking him up to being like every other man instead of the rare unicorn I thought he was, and I hadn't adjusted yet.

I'd like to blame how I felt to being hot off the heels of a murder, but I'm pretty sure that wasn't the trouble.

I'd really tried to be careful—to keep my feelings and fears in check—to go slowly, but daggone if Hobbs hadn't wooed me anyway. Daggone if he hadn't made me feel like there wasn't anything he wouldn't understand or that we, as a potential couple, couldn't overcome.

Daggone if he hadn't made me *trust* him. Or more accurately, I'd *let* myself trust him.

This morning, I felt empty and a little bit abandoned by Hobbs. Maybe that was because I put too much stock in his strength, in his constitution. Or maybe I was simply being too sensitive.

Nana nudged me with her cold nose. "Halliday Valentine? Answer me."

"Hush, Karen. Let the child mope. She's quite adept." Atti flew in and landed on the railing of Nana's corral to scold her.

I pointed at him with my red-gloved finger. "You hush, mister. I can mope if I want to. I've earned it."

Atti tsked me with a cluck of his tongue. "You haven't, Halliday. You've turned it into something it absolutely is not."

"Okay, you two, what the heck's goin' on? Is it about this murder bit last night?" Nana asked. "Are you sad you caught a killer? How can you be sad when you fought for justice?"

I leaned the rake on the stall and shook my head with a sniffle. "I'm not happy someone I never even considered turned out to be a murderer, but no. That's not why I'm *allegedly* moping."

Nana huffed, a puff of cold air whooshing from her nostrils. "Then what gives, kiddo?"

"Hobbs gives," Atti provided. "Our Halliday told him all about being a witch, and me, and even you, and rather than take into consideration it was a conversation worthy of some time to process for the poor bloke, Halliday's gone all doom and gloom."

"But why, Cupcake? Did he take it bad?"

I snorted and rubbed my hand over my grainy, tired eyes. "You know, that's the funny thing. He seemed fine until we got to you. When I told him you were my grandmother reincarnated in a reindeer's body, he got weird. Yet, he was perfectly fine when I showed him my magic. He had no problem with the bottle of wine I produced and when Atti talked to him, he seemed to take it in stride. But then I told him about you and suddenly, he had some urgent early meeting today and he had to go."

"*Oh*," was all nana said—and I knew the tone of that "oh." The tone said she knew something she didn't want *me* to know.

I cupped her muzzle with my hand and looked into her deep brown eyes. "Nana...what happened?"

She lifted her snout and attempted to look away, but I kept her gaze.

"Nana?"

She closed her eyes. "Nothing happened, child. Nothing at all."

Riiight. "Open your eyes, Nana."

She shook her head. "I got somethin' in 'em.

"You don't. Stop fibbing. What was that *oh* about? What did you do to Hobbs?"

"I didn't do anything *to* him, Sunshine. I like the boy. He's sure good-lookin', my Hot Sauce Hobbs, and he packs a mean carrot."

Atti snorted a laugh from his perch on her stall.

"Nana…" I said with a warning tone. "What do you know?"

She sighed, leaning back on her haunches before she said, "Listen, kiddo. He talks to me all the time. *All* the time. Comes in here every morning, lookin' like he's been up all night, and he talks. That's all. He just…talks."

My eyebrows lifted clear to my hairline. "About?"

"Oh, about lotsa stuff. Life, where he wants to go on vacation next year, how much he misses his mother now that she's gone, his work…"

She was purposely being evasive, and I knew it. Maybe she'd already told him she talks and the joke's on me?

"Aaand?" I prodded.

"Oh, fine. And *you*. That sweet boy talks about you, Halliday. He talks about you a lot, and now that he knows I can talk, too, he's probably losing his ever-lovin' mind, goin' back over all the chats we've had since he moved in and started dating you."

Now I was intrigued, and I knew what the answer would be, but I asked anyway. "What does he say?"

"Nope. Nuh-uh, young lady. He was telling me things without having any idea I could understand him. Talked to me all the time like I was some kind of pet or something—confided in me, etcetera. No way am I gonna be some kind of stoolie and rat that pretty boy out."

I laughed at her dramatic take on her conversations with Hobbs. "Nana, this isn't prison. You're not a stoolie and I'm not The Man."

"Well, I'm no snitch, either. So forget it. I respect Hobbs and I respect the chats we had, even if he thought they were one-sided. Once he found out who I am, he was probably embarrassed, for glory's sake. I mean, give the kid a break, Hal. He's been talking to a reindeer who's a reincarnation of your *grandmother*. He's told me private things I couldn't keep him from telling me for fear I'd let the cat out of the bag. You didn't want that, did you?"

"No," I mumbled, looking guiltily at my feet as though I were ten and had been caught stealing popcorn balls from the pantry.

"He probably hightailed it out of there because all our talks came rushing back to him in one big wave of confessions. Maybe he got a little embarrassed."

Confessions, huh? I wondered what he'd confessed? And why was he embarrassed? "You're probably right."

"Darn tootin' I'm right, young lady. Give him and me a break."

Nana was right, and I was out of line. I stroked her head and nodded. "You're right. It was rude of me to

16

ask you to out Hobbs, but you did make me feel better. Thanks for that, Nana."

She shuffled in her stall. "How so?"

I smiled at her and it was filled with love. "If Hobbs confided in you about something bad, if he was deceiving me or lying to me or he was saying something that would hurt me, I know you'd tell me no matter what. I think he was confessing how much he likes me, and that makes me feel better. But is that enough to make him okay with everything else?"

"If Hobbs is who I think he is, if all the talks we've had early in the mornin' are any indication of the kind of man he is, then I wouldn't worry your pretty head."

Taking a deep breath, I dropped a kiss on her head. "Thanks, Nana. I love you."

Nana nuzzled my palm and huffed. "I love you, too, kiddo. Now, how about a candy cane for my services?"

I dug around in my pocket and pulled one out, taking the wrapper off and breaking it in half. I held it up. "Just a half. We have to be careful about your sugar. Remember what the doc said."

She snatched it from my hand with her long tongue. "Yeah-yeah. Now git. I need a nap."

Looking at my phone, I realized I had to git, too. "I have to move it. I need to speak to Saul over at the lodge. He's still doing those cross-country ski tours through our land, and I wouldn't mind so much if it weren't for the fact that he and his tour skied all over some baby pear trees I just planted this past year.

They'll never survive someone's big, clompy feet, let alone skis and those pointy poles."

The Marshmallow Hollow Ski Lodge was just a bit east of my house, the only thing separating our acres a small stretch of land. Land where I'd tried to distinctly create boundaries by planting new pear trees next to the old ones and some arborvitaes on the border, and I was very careful to stick to the maps from the town.

It was interesting during peak season to see the ski lifts overhead and watch as people lost skis and all manner of skiing accoutrement. The owner, Saul Sanderson, sent someone out to collect the items and he was always apologetic.

Yet, every time someone new took over the ski tour guide position at the lodge—and that felt like quite often, because it was seasonal and the pay wasn't the greatest—I had to make a trip over and remind Saul that we had land deeds for a reason.

I wouldn't even mind his customers traipsing through my half so much if not for the fact that, not only did they trample my trees, they had this really bad habit of gawking in my windows. I imagine their curiosity gets the better of them when they see all the lights and decorations, and that would be fine, but a girl needs her privacy.

Once, I'd been getting out of my bathtub and found an elderly gentleman staring back at me—obviously on one of the moonlit tours the lodge offers. And he wasn't staring at me as in peeping intentionally. He was inspecting the lights on the tree outside my bathroom window—while I was buck naked and soaking wet.

When he realized he'd caught me in my birthday suit, he didn't bat an eye. Instead, he'd knocked on the window and asked where I'd purchased such unusual lights. All I can tell you is people have chutzpah and plenty to go around.

Things like that incident had happened on more than one occasion, and while I was all for the tourists who brought money to Marshmallow Hollow, and they were the reason we had such a bustling economy, I didn't want to help that economy while soaking wet and in the nude.

A fair trade, don't you think?

Anyway, I needed to get control of this before the winter really took hold and my new pear trees were decimated by eager cross-country skiers.

"I have to go, too, Nana I need to go over to the lodge and talk to Saul about those cross-country ski tours he gives."

"Are they trompin' all over stuff again?" she groused. "Honest, I don't want to deny a man his hustle, but land alive, he takes advantage."

I snickered. "His *hustle*, Nana? Where did you learn that expression?"

"Hobbs," she said with a matter-of-fact tone.

I rolled my eyes and shook my head with a chuckle. "Of course it was Hobbs. Okay, I need to shower and change. But I love you. Thank you for talking me down. I really needed that."

"You bet, Cupcake. You can always count on me."

I pressed one last kiss to her snout and left the barn with Atti flying behind me.

"I did tell you there must be a reason why your young man left so quickly, didn't I, Hal? Though, I admit, I'm quite jealous that he had adult conversations with Karen. All he could summon for me was the occasional coochie-coo."

I laughed as I went in through the mudroom and kicked my boots off, going in search of Barbra and Phil.

First a bit of unpleasantness at the lodge and then maybe I could talk Hobbs into lunch. A steaming bowl of chicken noodle soup I'd put in the Crockpot when I woke would hit the spot and might give us a chance to talk this through.

At least, I hoped that's what we'd do.

I hovered for a moment outside the ski lodge, watching as droves of tourists wandered in and out, snow clinging to their feet, their faces happy. Admiring the decorations, I noted some of our lights from Just Claus hanging in various places.

Saul had really outdone himself with the decorations this year. Even in bright daylight, they looked beautiful. He'd graced every window and door with fresh evergreen swags, draped with lights and pinecones. The wide automatic doors were flanked by two grand Christmas trees, full of ornaments in silver and gold.

He'd framed every doorway with icicle lights and an enormous sleigh was parked right in the center of the lobby, filled to the brim with decoratively wrapped presents in more silver and gold, and a waving Santa.

As I entered the lodge, I smiled at the enormous stone fireplace in the lobby—a lobby that looked more like a large, cozy living room with tartan plaid red and white chairs and big puffy gray couches.

I recognized Abel Ackerman from guest services, with his friendly smile and welcoming cardigan in red, dotted with snowflakes. He raised a hand to me in a wave before going back to whatever he was doing on his phone.

The scent of hazelnut coffee, redolent in the air, greeted my nose, along with the pastries Saul purchased fresh every morning from Dessert Storm.

I thought I might grab a cup of coffee, but then I spotted Saul at the desk and decided I needed to handle the business end of things first.

Weaving my way past a group of tourists from Asia excitedly having a conversation in their native language, I nodded politely at their smiling faces. Their colorful ski jackets grouped together as their guide led them out the doors toward the hill for tubing—a hill Stiles and I had spent a lot of time on as kids. Boy, were they in for a treat.

I got in line behind a couple from Germany, I think, judging from the one or two words I knew in German.

Tall and blond, they chatted happily, their faces red, likely from windburn on the slopes.

I loved the diversity the lodge and our tiny Christmas town brought to us. People came from all over the world to see Marshmallow Hollow at Christmas. I'd learned so much about different cultures just by meeting people at the ice festival and various events over the season. Seeing the usual varied crowd get bigger this year left my heart happy.

As I grew closer to Saul, I turned to take a peek at the small coffee area where guests could fill their own cups and grab complimentary pastries. Some of the waiters and waitresses from the dining room, in their plaid uniform shirts, were helping out, probably because it was so busy.

One of them lifted a heavy platter of apple fritters. Oh, glory be. My mouth watered thinking about Rhonda's apple fritters from Dessert Storm, crisp on the outside and gooey in the center, but I forced myself to stay on task.

I was here to give Saul what for because he clearly hadn't told his new instructor about our agreement.

"Halliday!" he called out, his white mustache rising at the corners as his cheerfully broad face broke into a genuine smile. "How are you, young lady?"

I loved his accent. He was what Maine was all about. Big, gruff, crusty around the edges with a heart of gold, hair the color of freshly fallen snow and ruddy skin from the cold. As he came around the desk, I gave

CARNAGE IN A PEAR TREE

him a quick hug, smelling Old Spice on his tan flannel shirt.

"Hey, Saul! Happy holidays. Looks like business is good."

He leaned back on the heels of his booted feet and grinned a wide smile. "Sure is. Best year yet. Hey, did ya grab a pastry? I made sure there are plenty this year. Last year we ran out. Man, that was some tussle."

I smiled and shook my head. "I'm good, Saul, but thank you."

He leaned an elbow on the edge of the desk, his puffy red vest spreading to reveal his barrel chest. "So what can I do ya for, kiddo?"

Shoot. I hated to bring him down when everything was going so well, but I had to draw the line somewhere. I couldn't keep showing my wares to all the tourists, and I certainly wasn't going to keep picking up their litter.

"It's about my new pear trees, Saul..." I said softly as the tinkle of happy Christmas music played in the background.

His broad shoulders sagged, along with his face. "Aw, heck, Hal. I'm sure sorry. Are the tourists wanderin' through there again? Dagnabbit, I told the kid where the line between our properties was! What is it about these youngin's these days? They need to get those dang phones outta their faces and open up their ears!"

Saul's cheeks went red in his exasperation, so I held

up a hand to soothe him. "It's okay, Saul. If you would just tell whoever the guide is to—"

But Saul wasn't listening, he was already on his cell phone, dialing someone. "Loretta? Send Troy to me, would ya?" he barked into the phone before he turned to me to explain. "This is what I get for hirin' family. My sister Janine's kid from Nebraska, right? Don't know his keister from his elbow, but boy that kid can ski."

Seconds later a sulky boy, tall and lanky with a white knit ski cap bearing the Marshmallow Hollow Ski Lodge insignia, slunk toward the desk, his long arms attached to hands stuffed into his thick down jacket.

"What up, Uncle Saul?" he asked, clearly not terribly concerned.

Saul's face went hard as he looked at the young man who was but maybe an inch shorter than is uncle. "Troy, this is Halliday Valentine, and here's *what up*, boy. She's the lady who owns the property right next to ours. Remember I told you about the line of pear trees that separates us and how you're not supposed to go past it with the ski tours because it's not ours?"

Troy shrugged, his youthful face indifferent. "Well, yeah. I guess. So?"

I thought Saul might explode. "You guess? So?" he repeated, his tone full of sarcasm. "You listen here, son. If you want this job for the rest of the season, you're gonna put your sorry behind in one of the lodge vans, drive over to Miss Valentine's house, and she'll personally show you where the line is. And I don't want to hear you crossed it again or I'm gonna send you back to your mama. You hear?"

Oh, geez. That's just what I needed. A broody teenager with a grudge. If I ended up having my house egged on Halloween, I'd know whose door to knock on.

Suddenly overly warm, I unzipped my bulky jacket and held up a hand. "It's all right, Saul. I just wanted you to be aware. He doesn't have to—"

But Saul stopped me cold when he held up his beefy hand, as well. "Nope. He's gonna follow you over there right now and he can take a picture of the spot with his almighty cell phone. Maybe then he'll remember what I told him—and replacing the trees is comin' out of his paycheck!"

Well, all right. Obviously, I wasn't going to change his mind. "Thanks, Saul."

His broad face changed on a dime as he smiled at me again. "You bet, Hal. Sorry again, kiddo. Now, you," he said, pointing to Troy, "get the van and skedaddle, then get back here for the afternoon tour."

Troy, his wide gray eyes sullen, looked to his uncle and held out his hand for the key. "Okay, Uncle Saul. Sorry…"

"Have a great holiday, Hal!" Saul scurried off to tend to the rest of his customers, leaving me with a pouty teenager.

Fighting a sigh, I said, "I'll meet you around front in my car, Troy. That work?"

He nodded but didn't say much, and I didn't try and make small talk because he looked positively miserable, and I thought Saul had been too hard on him already. Sure, I wanted him to stop trampling my trees, but he didn't have to pay for them.

I made my way past the crowd of incoming people, stopping as another group of tourists emptied from a bus and swarmed the lobby, leaving me in the thick of them.

Just as I turned, looking for another way out, I caught a glimpse of the coffee shop and made my escape. I could sneak out the back door and around to the front of the lodge, avoiding the mass of people.

I wormed my way past the crowd and managed to get to the entrance, where a swag of candy canes and ornaments adorned the doorway.

As I scooted inside, I stopped dead in my tracks, almost tripping over one of the café's chairs.

Well, well.

Know the reason Hobbs had to leave early last night?

To have coffee with a gorgeous blonde lady with legs up to her eyeballs and an expensive business suit made out of white silk.

CHAPTER 3

The pair of them looked very familiar with each other. It was in the way their bodies leaned in across the small table, the way she smiled at him with the tip of her tongue poking out between her white teeth. The way she bounced her high-heeled foot and swept her shoulder-length blonde locks behind her.

Hobbs, handsome as always, his beard trimmed to perfection, smiled back at her in a way I knew all too well.

I fought to catch my breath and avoid being seen, but my eyes were glued to them as I tried to process what was right in front of me.

That was the moment I decided I didn't want to process this at all. Of course, I didn't know what it meant, and I was trying not to jump to conclusions. I knew Hobbs was a good guy and he hadn't just run off to the arms of another woman the first chance he got because I'd freaked him out by telling him I'm a witch.

At least I didn't think so. But I didn't have time to find out. I had an errant, sulky teen waiting on me and some pear trees that deserved an end to their suffering.

I decided to turn back, but the crowd from the bus swarmed the café all at once, and there was no getting around passing Hobbs's table.

Unless I could duck behind the really tall guy with the rainbow knit hat, heading toward the counter.

Crouching, I inched around some tourists, shadowing the tall man's movements when I heard, "Hal?" above the hum of the crowd.

I only froze for a second before I kept it moving, pretending I didn't hear anything. And yes, it was childish. I should have simply walked up to them like an adult and asked who this blonde goddess was.

But I couldn't. My feelings were still a little raw after last night when Hobbs had left so abruptly. Besides, I wasn't even sure I wanted to *know* who this blonde goddess was.

Believe you me, I knew all about the classic romance novel misunderstanding. Goodness knows I'd read hundreds of them, and we weren't going to have one of those. Not today, Satan.

Today, I was going to run out of here like I was on fire and deal with the repercussions later. That's what I was going to do.

Immature? Maybe. But I like to think of it as being

cautious and prioritizing by not making Hobbs the sole purpose I existed.

As I was making my way to the back exit directly behind the tall guy, passing the gorgeous creature Hobbs sat with, I heard her say in a sexy voice, "Have you told her yet, Digby? It's long past time."

If I wasn't motivated to get the heck out of Dodge before, I sure was after hearing her words.

And as I skipped out the door as fast as I could without looking back, I wondered what exactly Hobbs hadn't told me...

In fact, I wondered that the entire way back to the house while Troy followed behind in the lodge's van, and all while I waited for him to hop out and follow me to the pear trees.

The ocean to the back of the house roared, and I could hear the frothy waves crashing on the cliffs at the end of our property. That almost always meant more snow.

"Hey, Miss Valentine?" Troy said as he made his way toward me, his lanky legs eating up the space between us in my driveway.

Tucking my freezing nose into my thick scarf, I kept trying not to think about Hobbs and the beautiful woman. "Uh-huh?"

"I'm real sorry about this. I promise to be more careful, but I can't afford to lose this job. I'm savin' up to buy a new board and I'll never make it if Uncle Saul fires me."

"You're a snowboarder?"

Suddenly, he beamed, his entire face lighting up. "Yep. Love it."

Now I felt worse. "I'm sorry, Troy. I didn't mean for Saul to take such harsh measures. I don't want you to pay for the pear trees, and I'll talk to your uncle about that and firing you. I just want you to be more careful when you take out the tours, okay? Maybe impress upon them that this is someone's home and hard work?"

He grinned wider, his lean cheeks brightening. "That's cool. You're cool. Promise I'll pay closer attention and it won't happen again on my watch."

I smiled at him, hoping to reassure him. "Then follow me, and be careful, the snow's pretty deep over here. You can take the picture your uncle wants you to take and then go off and do your thing."

He bobbed his head with another small smile.

December in Marshmallow Hollow was beautiful, but freezing cold with sometimes feet of snow. I loved it, but I didn't want to get stuck in it. Unlike Troy, I was no skier, cross-country or otherwise. Tubing and sledding were the extent of my winter sports.

As we neared the trees, I noted there were some discarded tissues, what looked like a receipt, and an empty cup from the lodge's café, making me sigh in distaste, but Troy bent and picked them up, detouring to drop them in one of my garbage cans by the garage.

The bitter cold of the day and the threat of more snow didn't deter me as I made my way toward the pear trees. I was determined to solve this problem and move on to the next one.

Hobbs.

If we were dating exclusively, who was that stunning, sunshiney blonde?

Ugh. This was ridiculous. I had to do the big girl thing and simply ask. I wasn't going to project or let my overactive imagination take over.

As we walked, I noted drops of something in the snow, but it was covered and muted by the light dusting we'd had last night. Maybe it was coffee drips from the discarded cup?

Ski lifts passed by overhead, and I cupped my hand over my eyes and looked upward at all the dangling feet, remembering how Stiles and I had taken lift after lift to tube down the slopes until our legs wobbled and we had no choice but to go home from sheer exhaustion.

I also remembered how our Christmas lights looked from all the way up there, and it gave me great pride to think the returning tourists could see I'd kept my family's tradition alive.

I stumbled while looking up, my legs still a little sore after last night's rumble in the field.

Was that only last night? It felt like a hundred years ago.

"Hang tight, Miss Valentine, and grab onto me. I'll help you," Troy offered with a smile.

I hooked my arm in his and we trudged through the deep snow until we were about fifty feet from the tallest of the pear trees—one that had been around since my nana was a new wife and mother to my mom.

As I was about to explain where the line for my property began, Troy stopped dead in his tracks, gripping my arm. "Miss Valentine, I don't think we should get any closer."

I squinted. "Why?"

He swallowed hard, as though he had a huge lump in his throat. "Don't you see what I see?"

"Huh? No, I don't see what you mean," I mumbled, letting go of his arm and moving a bit closer to the trunk of the tree.

"Wait, Miss Valentine—"

I gasped.

Oh. Oh, yeah. I saw it now.

Man. To have the eyes of the young, huh?

"Is that…is that what I think it is?" Troy stuttered, his voice becoming high and uncharacteristically squeaky.

"You mean blood? I think so, Troy."

In fact, as I crept a bit closer, I *knew* it was blood. All over the trunk of the barren tree and on the ground, rusty now from the light snow, and above it were some deep gouges in the tree, with what looked like hair stuck to them.

It looked as though someone had stabbed the tree trunk with something sharp and pointy, tearing at the bark.

What in the world had happened here—and for that matter, when?

I swung around, a chill racing up my spine as though someone might be watching me. Which was silly. I shook off the notion and held up my hand, hoping Troy understood he should stay back, because I was at a loss for words right now.

Maybe an animal had been injured? Or in a fight? But the gouges didn't look like scratches from an animal's nails, they looked like round holes in the bark, as though someone had poked at it over and over.

And if it were an animal, would it have been wearing a Marshmallow Hollow Ski Lodge plaid shirt…like the ones the waiters and waitresses wore?

And would it be torn and bloody at the base of the tree?

Though, there was no body. At least not in plain view—and you can bet I wasn't going deeper into the woods in search of one, either.

Nope. I'd had enough dead people for a while, thanks much.

Funny how I simply assumed there'd be a body when there was no actual proof someone had been killed. Evidence? Sure. A body? No. I was all murder and mayhem these days, wasn't I?

Though, why would someone's torn, bloody shirt be on the ground…?

The closer I looked, the more that pit in my stomach grew, and I knew what had to be done. There might not be a body, but there'd been carnage for sure,

33

and it needed investigating. On shaky legs, I fought to keep my voice steady when I all but ordered Troy to call the police.

"Call 9-1-1, Troy. Call them now and don't come any closer. We don't want to contaminate this if it's a crime scene."

"A crime scene?" he squeaked again.

"Call 9-1-1, Troy. Please!"

I heard him shuffle around behind me as I inspected even further, pulling out my phone to take pictures.

My sister Stevie, ace crime solver from the Pacific Northwest, said to always take pictures of the scene and never share them with anyone. Not even Stiles. If I wanted to amateur sleuth, I had to learn how to collect evidence on the sly, away from the prying eyes of the police.

It rather made me feel shady, but if I had a vision—which seemed to be the way every time there was a crime as of late—I wanted to understand what it was about instead of feeling my way around in the dark the way I had the last three times.

This last murder, I'd had visions of my new kitten, little Barbra Streisand, in a red sled, covered in blood, but I didn't necessarily relate it to the crime that occurred. Now, of course, seeing as everything was solved and tied up with a neat little bow, naturally the pieces of the puzzle of my vision fit, but at the time, nothing made any sense.

This time? This time I wanted to be prepared and

have a reference point. If Stevie said pictures could help, pictures I'd take.

As I clicked away as fast as I could, I heard the sirens from the police cars and then Stiles, calling my name.

"Hal?" he shouted, and I heard the panic in his voice.

As he ran toward me as best he could in the deep snow, three other officers followed, along with Sherriff Ansel Peregrine.

When Stiles stopped short in front of me, his burly body blocking out the glare from the gloom of the day, he grabbed my shoulders. "Are you okay? What's happening?"

I gripped his wrists to keep from shaking not only from the cold, but from such a gruesome scene. "I don't know." I shook my head and started over. "I mean, yes, I'm fine. My pear tree? Not so much."

He sighed a long sigh, the condensation from his breath making a puff of a cloud. "Did you have this poor kid call 9-1-1 because of a pear tree?"

"Don't be ridiculous, Stiles. You know me better than that. Of course not. Something happened here. Something bad. I just don't know what. I mean, take a look at the tree."

His eyes followed my finger to the tree and the bloody, torn shirt at the base. Stiles whistled. "That's a lot of blood…"

"And look at the holes in the trunk of the tree. And that shirt on the ground? It's a uniform from the lodge,

Stiles. It's the same one all the waiters and waitresses wear. Maybe even the gift shop staff, too."

That sent a shiver along my spine. A shiver of cold, ugly dread.

"The shirt has a nametag on it," he muttered distractedly as he pulled out his notepad and began scribbling notes.

I squinted against the glare of the snow. "Can you read it from here?"

Maybe I wasn't as paranoid as I'd first thought. What would a shirt from one of the employees of the lodge be doing here, bloody and torn, if someone hadn't been murdered?

But who? And why?

His sandy-brown eyebrows mashed together. "I can't, and even if I could, you know I can't tell you, Hal."

Ansel and the other officers ran up behind Stiles, looking at the surrounding area as they approached, their hands on their guns in their belts.

Ansel tipped his campaign hat at me, his face somber. "Hal," he said with a nod of acknowledgement. "What's happening?"

As I explained why we were here and what we'd come upon, Stiles furiously took notes and Ansel nodded a lot, only occasionally grunting, his big arms crossed over his chest.

"Anyway, I have no idea what happened. I didn't hear anything last night, if it happened then, and this morning I was at the lodge early. I guess whatever this is could have gone down while I was away."

I could always ask Atti or Nana if they'd heard anything during the night, but I'm pretty sure they would have mentioned it this morning.

Ansel nodded again, pulling his cell phone from his pocket. "I'll get a team out here as soon as I can, Hal. In the meantime, I'll have the guys cordon this area off." He looked at Troy. "That means no tours today, son."

Troy's face, shocked a moment ago, fell in disappointment, but he nodded and averted his eyes from the tree to look at Ansel. "Yes, sir. I'll tell Uncle Saul."

"Do you think someone was murdered?" I asked rather bluntly, the word sending another shiver along my arms.

We'd just finished wrapping up a murder and here we were again? It just didn't seem possible that our little town had turned into Grand Central Murder.

His muddy brown eyes scanned my face from under the brim of his hat. "I can't speculate, Hal, and you know it. Listen, I know you've become pretty durn good at solving mysteries these days, but not every case means murder."

That was fair, but also a little misguided. I mean, there was a torn shirt with blood on it at the base of the tree. I wasn't conjuring up a crime for the sake of having something to solve. Obviously, something had happened here. Something that involved blood and a sharp object, if the gashes in the tree were any indication.

"But what about the bloody shirt, Ansel?"

"A shirt with no body in it," he reminded me, and I wasn't sure if he was saying it out loud in order to keep me calm or if he was really convinced no crime had been committed.

I'm not sure why I was so adamant about proving he was wrong; of course he'd investigate either way. I think I needed something to focus on…anything that would take my mind off Hobbs.

I looked up at him, his face stern under the cloudy gray and purple sky. "So bloody, torn shirts show up and it's no big deal? C'mon, Ansel."

"I said I'd send a team out, Hal, and I will. I'll be sure they canvass the area and I'll send someone to the lodge to see if anyone's missing. Until then, I'd sure appreciate it if you'd go on inside and let us do our jobs."

"Like the good little girl I am, right? Go inside and shut my mouth and stop trying to play detective?" I asked, knowing it was huffy and I was lashing out in my frustration.

Ansel was a good guy, and he supported all of his wife Emmy's endeavors. *All of them.* He was all for equal rights for women, and I darn well knew it, but it appeared I was looking for a fight.

"You know what, Hal, I'm going to ignore that comment and ask you again to please go back inside the house—"

The next second or two that cut off Ansel's reply

will forever remain as vivid in my mind's eye as one of my visions.

From out of the sky, to the tune of the screams of the people on the ski lifts, a body fell into the most mature pear tree, knocking limbs every which way, which flew at our heads and faces.

The crack of the tree echoed in my yard, overriding even the crash of waves, crunching as it creaked with the weight of the poor unfortunate soul who'd fallen from the sky until it split down the middle and broke, dumping the body at our feet.

The *body*.

Well, I guess we had one of those now.

"Is that enough body for you, Ansel, or do you want it to rain arms and legs?"

CHAPTER 4

*A*fter that, we were all so stunned into silence, there was a moment when the only sound I heard was the beat of my heart and my pulse racing in my ears.

The person crashed through the limbs and fell, hitting the ground with such force, the impact virtually kicked up some of the solidly packed snow.

As the body slapped the earth, laid out like someone had hurled a frisbee to the ground, I thought my eyes might fall out of my head from shock.

My immediate reaction was to run to the poor person, thinking they must have fallen off the lift. At that point, I wasn't quite myself.

But Stiles stepped in front of me and stopped me with his big hands, gripping my shoulders. "Hal, don't."

Yet, I struggled against him. "What if they need help, Stiles?"

His tone was deeply grim when he spoke. "I don't think that's the case, Hal."

That's when I really studied the body and realization hit. A young man, his upper body naked, his eyes wide open and glassy, his mouth slack and sagging as though he'd screamed before dying.

His legs were bent and crooked, likely from the impact of the landing, and his arm was twisted so far behind his back, I was surprised it was still attached to his torso.

"Hal?" someone yelled. "Hal, are you okay?"

I turned to see Hobbs frantically digging his way through the deeper snow, each crunch of his steps making me more nervous.

I had just seen him with another woman and he'd left my house abruptly last night after I'd confessed some intimate details of my life. And now, there was a dead body in my side yard.

What was the definition of okay?

Suddenly, I didn't know what to say to him when he scooped me up in his arms and looked at me with concern in his bluer-than-blue eyes. "Hal?" he pressed.

Yes, man who has coffee with blonde goddesses?

"Are you okay? What's happening?"

"If a dead body falling from the sky in my yard is the stick we're measuring okay with, then I'm fine."

"*What?*" his tone rang out in disbelief, echoing through the yard.

I pointed behind me. Hobbs's neck twisted around. "What in all of…?"

Stiles wandered over to us and tipped his head at Hobbs. "How goes it, Dainty?"

"I might ask y'all the same. What the heck, Stiles?"

Stiles shook his head. "No idea, man. Troy, one of the kids who works at the lodge and runs the cross-country ski tours, called 9-1-1, and this is what we found. We're just beginning to investigate at this point."

He inhaled a breath as he looked at the tree and the body. "Hal? Are you okay? Did you see what happened? Talk to me."

I heard the concern in Hobbs's voice, but I was still feeling a bit shook up, not only from seeing him with the blonde lady whose name might as well be Flawless, but because a body had just fallen from a ski lift and dropped in my pear tree. It rendered me speechless and left me numb.

Shaking my head, I disengaged myself from his arms. "I don't know what to say. A body fell from a ski lift into my pear tree."

"Did you see anything?" he asked, gripping my shoulders and forcing me to focus on him.

I explained why Troy and I were here, and about finding the torn-up trunk of the tree and the shirt. "And then kablam. A body falls from the ski lift. That's all there is to tell."

Troy suddenly spoke up after clearing his throat. He moved nervously from foot to foot, his nose and cheeks red from the bitter cold. "Excuse me but, Miss Valentine, can I go, please? This is really freaking me out."

Stiles patted him on the back. "Sure. You go on back to the lodge, bud. But don't leave town, okay? We'll need a statement from you."

I nodded in agreement with Stiles. "You go right ahead, Troy. Be safe."

Troy was all but turning to run back to the lodge van when he seemed to remember something. "Sorry again about the trees, Miss Valentine. I swear I'll be more careful."

I gave him a sympathetic smile. He was only a kid. Seeing this had scared him and that made me feel awful. "It's fine, Troy. Go back to the lodge and warm up, okay?"

As though lost, he nodded. "Okay...um, bye." He stomped as fast as he could through the deep snow, his arms swinging as though they held a pair of ski poles.

"Poor kid," I murmured.

"You'd better go inside, Hal. The forensics team will be here any minute, swarming the place."

I nodded at Stiles in acknowledgement as he made his way over to the other officers. But before I left, with shaky fingers and my heart in my throat, I was going to take pictures of the body.

Just like my sister said to do.

"Hobbs? Would you go distract, please?"

He grinned and winked as though he hadn't been having a hot beverage with a hotter blonde. "At your service, little lady," he said, his Southern accent thickening.

I forced a smile at him, my lips chapped and

sticking to my teeth, and pulled my phone back out as he went to talk to the officers, surreptitiously snapping pics as fast as I could without getting closer.

The sound of more vehicles arriving said it was time to beat feet and let forensics do their job. I trudged through the snow, passing the forensics guys with a nod as I headed to the house.

"Hey, Hal!" Hobbs yelled. "Lemme change and I'll be right over, okay?"

I fought a roll of my eyes. Sure-sure. We were going to do the Cagney-and-Lacy-rides-again thing like he hadn't been having coffee with one of the prettiest creatures Marshmallow Hollow had ever seen?

Heck, she was even prettier than the previous Miss Marshmallow Hollow Christmas Pageant winner Trina Sommers, and that was saying something, because Trina was now a Paris runway model.

I also found myself fighting the urge to tell him to—as my sister's very British fiancé Win says—bugger off, because I didn't know if I *should* be telling him to bugger off or not. But I sure planned to find out.

And he'd better hope he gave me the right answer for who the perfect blonde lady was, or I was going to hex his parts unknown.

"So can you do magic, too?" I heard Hobbs ask Atti as he waited for me to change into some dry clothes. Having already done so, I sat on the edge of my bed, on my favorite puffy white comforter, cocking my ear to shamelessly eavesdrop.

"I do, Mr. Dainty," Atti drawled, his words dry as a bone.

"So if I asked you for a bacon cheeseburger, you could just make it appear?"

Atti's indignant tone rang in my ears. "This is not the Denny's, Mr. Dainty, and I am not a circus sideshow."

Hobbs's barked a laugh. "Naw. I didn't mean it like that, Atticus. I wasn't placin' my order or anything. I was just wondering where all the fancy food comes from. I mean, is Hal really that good of a cook?"

I narrowed my eyes as I jumped from the bed, scooping up Barbra Streisand and stomping down the hallway. "Yes, I'm really that good of a cook, and ps., my cooking skills came the hard way, Digby Dainty!"

"'Tis true, I frown upon Halliday using her magic for something she quite efficiently can make herself. When one lives amongst the humans, one must do as though in Rome—and human."

Hobbs gave me a sheepish glance as Stephen King sidled up to me, looking for love. "I'm sorry, honey. I did say I was going to ask questions and some might be dumb."

Now I was his honey? Last night he couldn't blow out of here fast enough, but today it was as though nothing ever happened.

"Yeah. You sure did."

I set Barbra on the floor to scurry after Phil and

made my way to the Crockpot on the countertop by the sink, where some homemade chicken noodle soup awaited me. Soup I'd made myself, thank you very much.

I took out a bowl and began to ladle some of the liquidy goodness into it when Atti buzzed in my face, his wings glowing in the Christmas lights strung along the counter.

"Halliday, surely you'll offer Mr. Dainty some soup?"

Hobbs was suddenly behind me, his eyes warm. "Yeah. Surely you'll offer me some soup, Halliday. I mean, I brought fresh-baked bread and everything. We have lunch together almost every day. You know the routine."

Without a word, I grabbed another bowl, filling that up, too, as Stephen King snorted at my feet.

Hobbs inhaled. "Smells awesome," he complimented me.

"And can you believe I made it with no magic at all?"

Hobbs clucked his tongue as he opened up the bread basket he'd brought and pulled out a cutting board from the drawer. "C'mon, Hal. I was just asking. What would *you* ask if you just found out your boyfriend was a...I dunno, vampire? Or a werewolf? Or a...a Gila monster?"

I couldn't help but snort a laugh at that ridiculous notion. "I don't think Gila monsters cook, vampires don't eat, and don't werewolves dine on livestock?"

Hobbs buttered me a slice of bread and handed it to me with a smile before making his way to my long wooden table. All very familiar events in our world as of late.

"I'm just sayin', I don't know what to ask. That's all. Last night you coulda knocked me over with a turkey feather, and all I've done since is think up one question as nutty as the next."

My eyebrows rose in question. "Is that why you blew out of here like a tornado? Or did it have to do with my grandmother and your early-morning chats, Texas?"

Might as well get it out in the open now.

Hobbs came around the table and cupped my chin, running his thumb over my bottom lip. "I wanna apologize for my hasty departure last night, Hal. Yeah, if I'm being totally honest, it did freak me out a little to learn Karen understands every word I've said to her and we've had one-way conversations I didn't know she could participate in. I think that's fair, don't you?"

I felt myself begin to soften at his light touch. "And you couldn't have told me that? Or texted me at least?"

"I should have, but honestly, I was real embarrassed, recalling all my blabbering at Karen. Regardless, I was wrong, and I'm sorry. I should have told you right then what was bothering me, but I guess Karen told you herself, huh?"

I tugged at his white cable-knit sweater with a lasciviously smiling Grinch on the chest. "She did, but

47

your secrets are safe with her. She won't betray your confidences."

He wiped a hand over his brow in dramatic fashion. "Phew. Anyway, speaking of things we need to talk about—"

Atticus flew between us, his wings fluttering a soft breeze between our faces. "Are you going to tell her who Trish the Dish is, Mr. Dainty?"

"Atti! Hush!"

Before changing, I'd told Atti about what happened by the pear trees and that I'd seen Hobbs with a gorgeous blonde at the lodge, having coffee, and what she'd said to him about telling me something.

I should have known better.

But Hobbs frowned, his expression filled with confusion. "Trish the Dish? I don't get it. Who's that?"

Atti buzzed into Hobbs's sightline. "The woman you were having a hot beverage with this morn, of course. Halliday saw you with her. Don't bother to deny it or I'll peck your eyes out, two-timer!"

"Atticus Finch!" I scolded. "Knock it off. Just this morning, wasn't it you who said I was overreacting to his abrupt departure last night?"

"That was before he was cavorting with a libidinous blonde bimbo!" Atti responded.

Out of the blue, Hobbs laughed his husky chuckle. "You mean the coffee at the lodge this morning?"

Stepping out of his arms, I crossed mine over my chest. "Yes. I saw you with that long-limbed, not-a-bottle-blonde in a silk suit, having coffee while I was there to talk to the owner about the trampling of my pear trees."

He pointed an accusatory finger at me with an amused smile. "So you *did* see me and you ignored me? Why? Because I was with Leona?"

Of course her name was something graceful and elegant like Leona. It wasn't something lame like my mother's weird play on words that had left me with the nickname for a man.

Ugh.

Still, I fessed up. "Yes. I pretended I didn't hear you because I didn't want to…to interrupt."

"Hogwash," Hobbs said, calling me out. "You were jealous. But there's no reason to be jealous. Believe me. And I planned to invite you to dinner tonight, with Leona there, so we can talk."

Now, curiosity had me by the tail. "About?"

"About something really important to me. But I guess we'll back-burner it because we have a crime to solve, right, Lacey?"

"You can't just tell me now?"

Hobbs ran a hand over his beard. "Leona's an important part of what I want to talk to you about, and she's going to be there for emotional support. She's not my sidepiece or anything like that, and never has been. I promise you'll understand better when we do talk, but it's not even remotely what you were thinking. I swear on my prize-winning Holstein, Susie, I'd never cheat on you. I like you way too much."

His words made my heart glow. So Leona wasn't a love interest or even an ex. Good to know.

"You had a prize-winning Holstein?"

He sat down in the chair and pulled his steaming bowl of soup toward him. "Yep. Won four 4-H contests with her, four years in a row."

I sat, too, dragging my laptop close. "Good on you. What's a Holstein?"

He chuckled his deep laugh and bit into his slice of bread with his white teeth. "It's a cow."

"So I guess you do kinda know what it's like to have a Karen."

He chuckled husky and low. "Um, no. Susie wasn't my reincarnated grandmother and she didn't talk."

I sighed wistfully. "I bet that makes owning a big animal so much easier."

"Because she wasn't my reincarnated grandmother?"

"Because Susie couldn't talk."

"I wouldn't tell Karen that," he said with a wink. "So, you ready to figure this out, Lacey?"

I pulled my phone from the back pocket of my jeans and slid it open. "Let's get to it, Cagney with the good hair."

Hobbs tsked-tsked me. "How many times have I told you to put a passcode on that? If someone steals your phone, they're gonna have a field day, honey."

I rolled my eyes at him. "If someone steals my phone, they're going to see pictures of a dead body and be so scared, they'll hand-deliver it back to me."

Hobbs laughed. "Please put a passcode on it."

"I promise I will. Now let's look at those pictures."

And just like that, for the moment, I let go of my anxieties about the beautiful Leona.

But I wasn't going to let them go forever. My curiosity had been piqued and it was itching my insides for answers.

CHAPTER 5

"*C*an you blow that up a little?" Hobbs asked, wiping his mouth.

I made the picture of the torn, bloody shirt with the nametag on it larger. "Can you read it?"

The nametag was situated at an odd angle. We both squinted and cocked our heads. "Looks like John or Jonah, maybe?"

Winning awards for photography was clearly off my table. Quite frankly, I stunk at taking pics.

I went to the lodge's website to see if Saul still did those cute little bios for the staff, then I reluctantly clicked on a picture I thought could be the dead man—or was he a teenager? I couldn't tell from the photo, but I'd bet a lung that shirt at the base of the pear tree was his.

"There he is," I said, pointing to the smiling young man, likely in his early twenties, with dark, inky hair and gray-blue eyes. His smile looked uncomfortable at best, and his eyes were dull and flat.

Hobbs bent and scooped up Barbra, tucking her under his chin to snuggle her. "He looks like a pocket fulla sunshine, huh?"

He did look unhappy—or maybe the word was annoyed, or even angry seemed suitable. "His name is Joey Scarpetti. He hails from Madison, Wisconsin, and he loves snowboarding, basketball, and coin collecting."

Hobbs grimaced. "Who kills someone who likes to collect coins?"

I shrugged and wondered that myself. It was definitely an innocuous hobby. "We don't even know if he was dead before he fell off the lift, do we? Maybe the tree has nothing to do with Joey."

"You don't really think he got on the ski lift with no shirt, do you? It's freezing out there. He's from Wisconsin. He knows winter."

"True," I acknowledged as I looked closer at the picture of Joey's body. "If only I took better pictures, we might be able to tell what type of stab wounds they are, but I was trying to get them on the fly. They're a little blurry, huh?"

"I'll admit you're no Annie Leibovitz, but you were in a rush, honey."

I stared off at the fireplace, where Stephen King had taken his usual place in a warm bed with a fuzzy blanket, and decided social media might be the ticket. "I think Facebook is our next stop."

Social media played a huge role in us catching our first killer. Or was it our second? I can't remember. Either way, it was a fount of information on many occasions, but it appeared Joey didn't have a Facebook page.

Who, at the ripe old age of at best maybe twenty-five, didn't have a Facebook page? Or had Facebook become too MySpace for the kids these days?

I checked Twitter, Instagram and even TikTok, and if Mr. Scarpetti had a social media presence, it was under another name.

"So we have a dead kid with no shirt and no social media," Hobbs said.

Cupping my chin in my hand, I couldn't help but smile at Hobbs as he stroked Barbra's soft gray fur and she purred like a sports car motor. "Well, I guess we don't know for sure it was his shirt."

"He," Hobbs said, pointing to one of the pictures on my laptop screen, allegedly of Joey Scarpetti alive, "definitely looks like *him*." He pointed to the image from my yard.

I got up and took a peek out the windows facing the side of the yard where I'd left the forensics team to see if they were still processing, only to find them loading the body into the ambulance.

There was yellow crime scene tape everywhere, and as the clouds began to thicken and the ocean roared, I shivered. It was almost Christmas, a time when we should all be taking part in community activities, enjoying potluck meals together, decorating and watching holiday movies. Instead, we were faced with yet another murder in our small town. I grabbed my chair and sat back down.

The ominous feeling of death, thick in the air, took hold of my throat.

And that was when it happened. The world slowed down, crawling to an almost tangible halt. My body felt sluggish, as though I were walking through mud, my limbs heavy, the sound of my heartbeat in my ears…

Before me, there was that dang typewriter again, sitting all alone in a room with nothing more than four walls.

What? What are you trying to tell me, universe?

And then everything changed. The world tilted, the typewriter melted away as though someone had turned it into hot candle wax, slipping off the table and onto the floor to drip in a glistening black puddle.

Then there was laughter. Tinkling female laughter, floating through the air from behind a white door, followed by a male's chuckle.

I knew it would do me no good to attempt to open the door to see who was behind it, but I tried lifting my arm anyway, to no avail. I was always useless during a vision, and my arm alone felt like it weighed a hundred pounds.

But I didn't have to open the door. It swung open so violently, it slammed against the light blue wall.

A young woman flew out of the room, her long hair, almost burgundy, clinging to her face as she sobbed.

Lift your head! I wanted to yell. *Let me see your face!*

But instead, she ran back into the room. I'm assuming it was her bedroom—there were fluffy purple pillows on the full-size bed and a small white teddy bear with a missing eye in the center of a rainbow-colored quilt. Her vibe felt like the space was very familiar to her.

With her back still to me, she grabbed her laptop and held it high with a tormented scream before throwing it to the floor and watching it smash.

And then as she sobbed, her shoulders shaking, her cries ragged and agonizing, she grabbed her purple and white shoulder bag and yanked it open, pulling out a bottle of pills. A bottle I couldn't see very clearly no matter how hard I tried to focus.

No. *No! No! No!* I wanted to scream, knowing her intent as she looked at the clear orange bottle. I *knew* what she was about to do. I tried to scream, *I'll help you. I'll listen! Please don't!*

But of course she couldn't hear me, and inevitably, I couldn't stop her from pouring a handful of the pills into her palm and pushing them into her mouth.

She followed them up with a glass of water from her nightstand and then she lay down on her rainbow-quilted bed, grabbed her teddy bear and closed her eyes.

I can't tell you the impending sense of doom and heartbreak I felt at that moment. As though someone's whole world had just collapsed and I'd watched it happen without preventing it.

Tears fell down my face in frustration and anguish, my body trembled and my pulse raced.

Then there was a large palm running soothing circles over my back and a whiskey-warm voice whispering in my ear. "Hal, I'm here. It's okay, honey."

Hobbs's voice soothed me, pulling me back from the edge of an abyss of helplessness.

I fell toward him, he caught me to keep me from hitting the floor. He caught me the way he always did when I had a vision. My muscles finally started to release and Hobbs grabbed my hand. He pulled my clenched fist to his chest and uncurled my fingers, massaging the digits until I relaxed. "This was a rough one, huh?"

My temple throbbed. "It was the worst," I replied, trying to keep a sob from escaping my lips even though I felt the stain of wet tears on my face.

"Lemme get some antibiotic cream to put on your palms. Be right back." Making sure I could sit, he dropped a kiss to my damp brow and went off to the bathroom.

Atti buzzed to the table, hopping on my forearm and clucking his tongue with clear admonishment. He jabbed at the soft heel of my hand with his tiny beak. "Oh, my sweet Halliday. Look at your hands. Shall we discuss, or is it too soon?"

I blinked as I looked at the half-moon shapes my fingernails had dug into the palms of my hands.

Atti was asking the wrong question.

The question was—was it too late? Had this vision

57

already happened? Could I prevent it from happening if it hadn't already? My stomach turned and twisted into a tight knot of terror.

I'd never witnessed someone attempting to leave this world. Never in life and never in a vision. Sure, I had all sorts of visions, past, present, future. Some worse than others, but never one where I wondered if the person involved needed saving.

My heart began thumping with the beat of a thousand drums. The sound canceled everything else out as I tried to remember any detail that could help me figure out where this vision stood, but nothing came to me.

The prescription bottle... If only I'd looked harder. It could have been a clue as to what the name of the woman was or what the date had been.

Hobbs sat back down and wiped my cheeks with a tissue. "Are you ready to talk about it, or do you need time to process?"

Hobbs understood these dang visions of mine. He understood, he accepted, and most of all, he supported me. That realization hit me square in the nose and I clung to it for comfort, letting it erase any residual anger over Leona.

I trusted Hobbs. Whatever he had to tell me, he'd do so when he was ready. No one understood that more than me.

Until then, I absolutely had to figure out who this woman was and if her plan to leave this world had succeeded, or if there was a way I could prevent it.

It left me filled with urgent anxiety.

I didn't know if it had anything to do with the crime we'd stumbled upon today. I've had lots of visions that have nothing to do with crimes, but the niggling feeling that this girl and the man who'd fallen from the ski lift were connected stuck in my craw, and I had to do something.

With a determined swipe of the tears from my eyes, I said, "I'm ready to talk about it."

As I explained the vision, Hobbs applied antibiotic cream to my palms, which was completely unnecessary, but seemed to soothe him as much as it did me.

"So this woman...you think she was going to..." Hobbs couldn't say it any more than I could, but I had to if I were going to face this head on.

"Take her life," I said bluntly, the words catching in my throat. "I *know* she was going to. What else can taking a handful of pills mean, Hobbs? And her vibe? It was tortured, tormented, whatever word that best describes someone on the very edge of the cliff—that was what I felt. I definitely think she was trying to harm herself."

"But you didn't see any relation to today's mess in your yard?"

"No. Nothing obvious, but I *feel* it, Hobbs. I feel it here, in my gut."

He pushed a strand of hair from my face. "I guess it does me no good to tell you that resting after such a horrific vision might be a good idea."

I leaned into him and rested my head on his shoulder. "You already know the answer to that."

The look he gave me was resigned. "Then we need to beat feet, Cowgirl. Let's go to the lodge and do what we do best—poke around, ask questions about Scarpetti, get on everyone's nerves."

I smiled at his handsome face, even though my chest was fraught with tension. "You're okay, Texas."

"Even though I had coffee with...what did you call her? Not-a-bottled-blonde?"

I made a face at him as I scooped up Barbra and dropped a kiss on her fuzzy head. "With long legs. She has long, long legs, and you're riding a fine line, buddy. You'd do well to remember who has the magic in this relationship," I teased.

"I feel like I've been threatened."

I turned to head to the mudroom where I had a fresh jacket and dry boots awaiting me. "Don't make me send my broom after you, Cowboy!" I called.

"Do you really have a broom?" he asked. "Does she really have a broom, Atticus?"

I laughed, and I was still laughing as we headed over to the lodge in his Jeep.

CHAPTER 6

"So, where do we start?" Hobbs asked when we entered the lodge, the warmth of the fireplace welcoming, even if every single guest appeared to be in chaos. People milled about in crowds, some wringing their hands with worried looks on their faces. Some looking confused and displaced.

Suddenly, the enormity of what we'd set out to do hit me full on. I grabbed his hand and squeezed. "What if…what if we're too late? Or we don't figure it out and that woman…"

Hobbs pulled me tight to his side. "Don't project, honey. One moment at a time, okay? Let's stay focused and figure out if your vision is even connected to what happened today. We'll keep busy by figuring this out, okay?"

That made me feel a bit better. Keeping busy was always a way to find some small measure of solace.

Still, I felt a little lost about where to begin, but

Hobbs took my hand and pulled me toward the crowded desk area. "To start, let's just open our ears and listen."

I stood on tiptoe and whispered in his ear, "You mean, eavesdrop. The horror."

He grinned, pulling off his knit hat with the light-up reindeer on it. "Yup."

So we mingled, moving around some tourists from Japan and a group from France who spoke their native language, leaving Hobbs and I little choice but to move on because neither of us spoke French.

But we hit paydirt with a group of kids who sat on the big couches by the fireplace. According to one hysterical woman we'd passed, who was complaining to her husband, the police had ordered everyone to stay inside the lodge until further notice.

The kids were like cooped-up animals, forced to stay inside with no activities to keep them busy.

Hobbs pulled me close and wrapped an arm around me, our backs to the couch while the kids talked.

"Holy crap, dudes!" a boy with a youthfully excited voice said. "Did you hear that guy who worked in the kitchen got whacked?"

Another one of the kids, a young girl, said, "Shut up, Hudson! Have some respect for the dead. God, you're a jerk. I can't believe Mom and Dad made me come on this trip with you. I could be home with my friends, going to ice skating socials and holiday parties, and instead I'm here with you and your big, stupid mouth!"

As you know, I was an only child. Hearing the

siblings argue made me smile, and it also gave us a better idea of who was dead. A guy from the kitchen.

"*You* shut up, Galinda. You just wanted to stay home so you could make kissy face with your crater-face boyfriend!" her brother accused with a youthful voice.

The couch shifted as Galinda jumped up and yelled at her brother. "Oh, my God, I hate you, Hudson! And you better shut your face, or I'll tell Mom and Dad what you were doing, creeping around the lodge last night. Weirdo!"

"Guys! Knock it off. Something really bad happened. It's not a time to be acting like a bunch of immature babies. Joey was *killed*. He was a nice guy, and he always gave me extra dinner rolls," a voice of reason said. "Stop being so disrespectful. This isn't some cop show, you idiots. You can't just turn it off and forget it. This really happened. There really is a murderer on the loose!"

I desperately wanted to turn around to see what these kids looked like, but Hobbs must have sensed it and shook his head, and he was right. I didn't want to break their rhythm.

At least now we knew Joey Scarpetti was indeed the one who'd been killed.

Another female voice, more mature than the others, chimed in with an ominous statement. "I heard the police say he was dead before he fell from the ski lift. So yeah, duh, murder. All I know is, I wanna go home. Nothing says Merry Christmas like a dead guy."

I had to agree with her. If I were a teenager, the last

thing I'd want to do is stay at a place where a murderer was on the loose, no matter how good the tubing.

"How long are we stuck inside here, anyway?" another teen asked. "I wanna tube on the big hill today. The snow's awesome right now. Man, this sucks."

Ah. I remembered well the big hill. Stiles and I had tubed down that a hundred times as kids.

"Guys!" A cheerful voice entered the conversation— one that reminded me of a cruise director, complete with a clap of hands. Peppy and light. "I think I can help. I'm Clarissa, and I'm the events coordinator here at the lodge, and if you'll all get permission from your parents, then follow me, I've got some super cool activities lined up for you!"

I had to turn around. The spell was broken anyhow. They weren't going to gossip with each other with an adult there, and I was dying to see the kids' faces when they responded to Clarissa.

"Can we go tubing?" one boy, a tween if I was guessing correctly, asked.

The short but spunky young woman, her chestnut hair in a high ponytail, her face clear-skinned and glowing, shook her head with a grin. "Nope, but I have stuff that's just as cool! C'mon, go talk to your parents and let's get a leg up!"

Every last one of them rolled their eyes and their shoulders drooped as they scattered to ask permission from their parents.

On impulse, I hopped in front of Clarissa and stuck out my hand. "Hi there. I'm Hal Valentine, Clarissa."

She grinned. "Oh, right. The lady who owns the Christmas factory, right?"

Cocking my head, I pulled off my hat and asked, "How'd you know?"

"How many people do you know with the name Halliday Valentine? Besides, the factory's legendary around here, and so is your reindeer, Karen."

Huh. I forgot sometimes that my nana had made quite a splash in town, mooching off the kids for candy canes.

"Would you mind if I ask you a question about Joey Scarpetti?"

In a flash, her cheerful face went from light to dark as she ran a hand over her high ponytail. "What about him?"

I tucked my hat in my jacket pocket and tried to look casual. "Did you know him, Clarissa?"

Her eyes shifted to the floor. Gone was the cheerful façade. "I wanted to, if that counts for anything. I tried to get his attention—believe me, *I tried*," she reiterated, in the way a woman does when she's discovered the man she's attracted to isn't returning the favor. "But he gave off a not-interested vibe pretty quick. So I backed off, because boundaries are boundaries."

"Do you think he had a girlfriend?" Hobbs asked the question I planned to be my next. If my vision was connected, maybe the woman was Joey's girlfriend.

She shrugged, her ponytail swishing. "I dunno. If he did, he never said so."

"Did he ever talk to you about having any trouble

with anyone here at the lodge? Did he ever argue with anyone?"

She pushed her hands into her khaki trouser pockets and shook her head. "Not that I saw. Everyone liked him because he was so drama free. Plus, he was really polite, a hard worker, and all the guests loved him."

We were off to a great start, weren't we? "Well, if you remember anything, would you text me, please?"

She slapped that cheerful smile back on her face, even if she looked a little confused, and said, "Sure. Just put your number in my phone."

I did exactly that and handed it back to her. "Thanks for talking to us, Clarissa." We turned to leave but she stopped us by reaching out and touching my shoulder.

"Miss Valentine? Wait! I just remembered something. Sorry. It's been a crazy day. I don't know if it means anything, but Joey was asking the head of housekeeping about a specific room here. He was pretty frustrated because Millie's partially deaf, and she didn't have her hearing aid in that day and was having trouble answering his questions. He raised his voice with her. I mean, he apologized right away, but it was super strange to see him get so excited because he was always such a cool cucumber."

Again, Hobbs took the questions I was going to ask. "Did he say why he wanted to know about the room? Or *what* he wanted to know about the room? Was anyone else around to hear this go down?"

"No. It was just me. It happened a couple of days ago, I think. Time's sort of been a blur since the holiday crowd arrived. Millie got so upset, she ran off before he got an answer. I just remember thinking it was so strange that Joey wanted to know about someone who'd stayed in a room, and to get so upset when he couldn't get his point across to Millie. She's as sweet as can be. But like I said, I don't know if it means anything."

If I wasn't already confused enough, this added to my confusion. All I kept hearing was how nice Joey was, but he was upset at a woman who was partially deaf? Joey had secrets...and I wanted to know what they were.

"Where is Millie?" I asked. "How can I find her to speak to her?"

"She had a doctor's appointment today, but she'll be in later this afternoon. I'll tell her you want to talk to her," Clarissa offered, looking at her phone. "Listen, Miss Valentine, I have to go. I've got a lot of antsy kids on my hands who aren't thrilled about not being able to leave the lodge. I've got to try and find a way to amuse them until my shift is over."

Immediately I nodded, smiling in sympathy. "You go, Clarissa, and thank you for your help."

"Bye," she called as she ran toward the lodge's rec room.

"Welp, that was at least a little bit of help."

"Guess we have a date with Millie later today, huh?"

I agreed. "I guess we do, and at least now we know

for sure it was Joey Scarpetti who fell off the lift, he worked in the kitchen, and he'd left this world before he landed in my yard."

Hobbs winked, his neatly trimmed beard lifting with his smile. "See? A clue already, and all we mostly had to do was stand around. C'mon, Lacey, let's keep moving toward the kitchen. Who knows what we'll hear over the soup of the day?"

I hooked my arm through his and followed him to the café, where the kitchen was located. "Just so happens, I have a connection in the kitchen."

"Oh yeah? Who?" he asked as we stepped around people in snow jackets and heavy boots.

"Willow Sinclair. Her aunt Agnes works at Just Claus in the lights department. She's the chef here."

"Then let's see if we can find Willow."

The café was swarming with people, all looking as concerned as the guests out in the lobby. The scent of coffee was still fresh, and empty plates and bowls sat on the tables, obviously from the lunch service.

The waiters and waitresses scurried about and the busboys gathered dishes, but the mood, despite the cheerful Christmas music and decorations, was somber at best.

I peeked into the window of the swinging doors to the kitchen, where several of the employees stood around in their white aprons, their eyes helpless and lost. I located Willow by the big stainless-steel sinks, her shoulders slumped, her arms crossed over her chest.

I caught her attention with a wag of my finger and a tap to the window. She raised a hand to wave at me, pushing off from the sinks and walking across the room to push open the kitchen doors, her face brightening a shade.

"Hal! Merry Christmas! How are you?" she greeted me warmly, giving me a quick hug scented with cinnamon and freshly baked bread. "Auntie Aggie was just talking about what a great boss you are and how much she loves the month of December off to spend with family and friends."

I grinned. Agnes Sinclair was a real card at sixty-two, and I adored her—she was my soul mate in all the ways of colorful language. She cussed like a sailor, and I loved it.

"She's a valuable employee and she works hard all year long. She deserves the time off. They all do, if you ask me. They work hard leading up to the holiday, and I appreciate them."

Hobbs stuck his hand out. "Hobbs Dainty. Pleasure, ma'am."

Willow grinned and winked, her cheeks pink as she twisted her long braid of ginger hair between her fingers. "Oh, I've heard all about you. You're Hal's new beau—and a Southern beau from Texas to boot. A real cowboy, huh?"

He chuckled. "I am indeed Hal's boyfriend. Real nice to meet you."

"Anyway, Willow," I said, sobering. "How are *you*? I

heard the man who was killed was one of your kitchen staff?"

She gripped her temples with her index and thumb and squeezed. "He was. His name is...was, Joey Scarpetti. He was new, but he was really good at his job. One of the best of the staff, actually, and certainly one of the best waiters I've ever had."

I grabbed her icy fingers and squeezed. "I'm so sorry, Willow. Is there anything I can do?"

Her full face became stricken with fear as she wiped her other hand on her mussed white apron. "Can you tell me who would do this? It's terrified us. We're afraid to do *anything*, knowing someone's running around out there who's a murderer."

I found myself launching into the usual questions. "Did Joey have any trouble with anyone? An argument, maybe? Did he seem distressed?"

She leaned into me so she couldn't be overheard. "I don't know about any arguments, but he definitely kept to himself. He did his work, he was always pleasant to the guests, and at the end of his shift, he went back to the bunkhouse and that was that. He was a good kid who never made trouble. I told the police the same thing when they questioned us. Everyone who works in the kitchen pretty much told them as much, too. He was just a nice guy."

The bunkhouse was for the employees who came from out of state. Saul had a work program where kids from all over the country could experience hotel management and all aspects of running a successful business in the hospitality industry.

He did it twice a year, when the tourist seasons were at their heaviest. During the fall for the foliage, and the winter.

We did it at Just Claus, too, when things got hectic just before we closed down in December and we needed the extra help.

"I'll let you get back to work, Willow. It looks like you have your hands full, but if you think of anything, text me, would you please?"

Willow smiled, her round face lighting up. "Of course I will. Hey, I heard it happened at your place. Is it true? Did he really..." She blanched and swallowed hard. "Did he really fall from the ski lift?"

I blew out a breath and forced the vision of Joey's body landing at me feet from my mind. "He did."

Her expression went stricken. "Oh, Hal, I'm so sorry you had to see that. How awful for you."

I didn't want to dwell on the actual event. I couldn't. Mostly because it was disturbing, but also because I really wanted to find out who the woman in my vision was and if it was possible to stop her from what she planned to do. If I hoped to do that (I prayed I could do that), I had to keep moving.

Giving her a quick hug, I patted her back. "It's okay, Willow. Listen, if you hear anything, text me, call, whatever, okay?"

"Sure thing. I hear you're the woman of the hour these days, Miss Crime Solver."

My cheeks flamed hot and I grew flustered. "I'm absolutely not. I just got lucky."

She cocked her head, her look skeptical. "*Three* times? Is that luck or skill, miss?"

Wagging a finger at her, I jokingly scolded, "Oh, you. It's not what you think. Anyway, keep me in mind. And hey, tell Agnes this fellow potty mouth misses her and hopes she's enjoying her time off. Can't wait till the new year so we can share a coffee break and the latest swear words she's learned on TikTok."

Willow saluted me and nodded with a smile. "You bet, Hal, and if anyone else finds out something or hears something, I'll send 'em to you."

But I shook my head, even if I was feeling a small sense of pride that she'd noticed I'd sort of solved a couple murders. "Send them to the police first."

"Why would I do that when you're the one who keeps solving all the mysteries in Marshmallow Hollow?" she asked. "You're a far better bet, my friend, if you ask me. Now, I gotta get back to work. If I don't see you, have a great holiday, Hal...and Cowboy." Using her chubby hand, Willow pushed her way back into the kitchen.

Hobbs smiled his devastatingly handsome smile. "Look at you, Detective Lacey. A real superstar, right here in little ol' Marshmallow Hollow."

I flapped a hand at Hobbs and dismissed the notion. "You shush. I'm no such thing. I didn't really figure much out. I sort of stumbled onto stuff like some clumsy Keystone Cop. That's what I did. I got lucky.

Now, no more talk about me. Let's keep it moving, Texas."

As I turned to head back toward the lobby, a young woman I didn't recognize approached. Blonde with blue-tipped ends to her hair, she looked at me with worried eyes as she took quick strides in my direction.

"Are you Halliday Valentine? The lady whose yard Joey— Who owns the property where he fell off the ski lift?"

"I am. Who are you?" I asked as gently as I could, but my clue radar was on full alert.

She twisted her fingers together in a tangle of digits. "I'm Sierra Murphy. I work the front desk. I heard you talking to Willow, and I remembered something I think could be important. Or maybe. I mean, I don't know. But I figured I'd better tell someone."

"Have you told the police what you know yet, Sierra?" Hobbs asked.

She gave him a vague smile, leaning back against the walnut paneling, her pale skin standing out against the dark backdrop. "Not yet. Though, I promise I will as soon as possible. But I keep hearing you're the crime solver in town, so I figure if it helps, you should know, too. I mean, I don't even know if it's going to make a big difference anyway."

Sure. I was a real crime solver. Saying that was like saying Hiroshima was just a little dust cloud. "So what can I do for you, Sierra? How can I help?"

Her eyes got a faraway look as she glanced past my shoulder at all the people in the café. Nibbling at her nail, when she finally spoke, her words were nervous and shaky. "Joey was always so quiet, but he was friendly, you know? He mostly kept to himself but sometimes he'd have lunch with some of us, and he was kind of funny."

"I've heard that from everyone," I revealed. "That he was a nice guy, but quiet and a really hard worker.

Tightening her green sweater around her small waist, she shook her head. "He was, and I don't know if what I heard that day means anything, but because Joey was so quiet and nice, I guess it just seemed strange. But it didn't really stand out to me until today, when I heard...well, you know."

I reached for her hand and gave it a small squeeze to reassure her she was among friends.

"Anyway, he was on the phone with someone named Sabrina, and he was *really* upset. He said, 'Don't worry, Brina. I won't let it get any further. They won't get away with it. I'll make sure it gets erased. All of it. Every last bit. I promise.'"

Le gasp!

I think we finally had a legit clue.

Holy shitake mushrooms.

CHAPTER 7

Sierra's words sent a cold chill up my spine and down along my arms.

Erased? What did that mean? Did it mean *anything*?

"Is there more, Sierra? Did he say anything else?"

Her cheeks puffed outward when she blew out a breath. "Nuh-uh. When he saw me, I think he figured I heard him, I guess. So he walked off to another part of the lobby to finish his conversation. But those were his exact words. Like I said, I don't know if it meant anything or even if it's important to the investigation. For all I know he could have been talking about anything, but he sure sounded pretty upset. Joey wasn't a guy who riled easily. He was really calm and easygoing, but that phone call was just..." Sierra shrugged. "It was just a *different* Joey. I'd never seen that side of him. So...intense, I guess would be the right word."

Okay, so who was Sabrina? A Girlfriend. Friend? Family?

"Do you have any idea who Sabrina could be, Sierra?" Hobbs asked, his voice rife with concern.

Her head vehemently shook in the negative. "No. No, sir. None. He never talked about a Sabrina. He didn't talk about much at all that had to do with his home life."

But this begged the question, how well did Sierra know Joey? "How long did you two work together, Sierra?"

"About a week or so. He got here for the hospitality work program about the same time I did."

Was that enough time to really know if Joey's demeanor was always quiet and easygoing? A week wasn't much time to really know anyone. Sometimes a lifetime wasn't enough, but a week was hardly any time at all.

Still, everyone said the same thing about Joey Scarpetti. He was nice, a hard worker, quiet and easygoing. Yet, he was an odd duck in that he didn't exist anywhere on social media.

Didn't they say that about killers? He was so quiet? I mean, Jeffrey Dahmer was quiet and look what happened there.

But Joey wasn't a suspect in his own murder. It simply struck me as so strange that everyone had an identical opinion of him. It felt purposeful. As though he wanted to remain nondescript for a reason.

"I definitely think you should tell the police, Sierra. My best friend works for the Marshmallow Hollow Police

Department. His name is Stiles Fitzsimmons. If you'll give me your phone, I'll put his number in your cell and you can contact him with the information you have. Okay?"

She nodded and pulled her phone from the pocket of her green sweater, handing it to me. As I tapped in Stiles's number, she inhaled sharply. "Wait! I just remembered something else. Oh, I can't believe I forgot this part!"

I frowned. "What's that?"

"When Joey was walking away and telling Sabrina not to worry, he said he found an awesome purple Christmas ornament he'd bring to her when he came home. Almost like he was trying to make her feel better, and the color purple would do it."

I froze at those words, and Hobbs stiffened beside me.

Purple.

The girl in my vision had a purple bedroom with purple pillows and a purple and white purse.

I *knew* my vision was somehow connected to Joey's death, and now I was more convinced than ever. We needed to talk to Stiles right away.

———

Stiles looked tired when he met us at the café. We waved him over to our table and flagged the waitress to grab him a cup of coffee and a sandwich.

It was mostly empty now, with the exception of two

or three couples, the cheerful Christmas music louder without all the chatter from the guests.

He slid into the red vinyl chair opposite me at our small, round table with a miniature Christmas tree in the center. "Afternoon, guys. You two okay after this morning?"

"Forget us, how are *you,* buddy?" Hobbs asked. "You look like a wet noodle."

Stiles ran a hand over his face and the stubble forming on his chin. "It's been a hectic day from the minute I put my feet on the floor at five a.m. So what's up? You guys been snoopin' around? Got somethin' for me?"

I told him about my vision and the woman in it and the connection I thought there was between her purple room and Joey Scarpetti.

He reached across the white Formica table and grabbed my hand. "Man, Cupcake, that sounds pretty scary. You all right?"

"I'll be okay when we find out who she is. I'm terrified I won't find her in time, Stiles. I have to try and find her."

Stiles leaned back against the chair. "Then you don't know if this has happened yet?"

I fought the sudden onslaught of tears. "No," I whispered, trying to keep my voice even. "But I need you to let me help you, Stiles. And I need you to help *me* and give me all that sensitive police information you say you can't share with me when you're investigating, because I won't be able to live with myself if I don't try and figure out if I can stop this and something happens to her because I didn't get there in time."

As the waitress dropped off his egg salad sandwich and coffee, he gave me a sympathetic look. "That's a lot of pressure to put on yourself, Hal. If this has already happened, there's nothing you can do."

I sat up straight in my chair and looked directly at him. "And if it hasn't? Do I want to look back and say if only I'd done something? I can't live with that."

Stiles's reaction said he was going to tell me no, but I cut him off. "Stiles, you know my visions are real, and you know I would never, ever betray your confidence. No one has to know you're giving me information. I swear I won't utter a word."

He wiped his mouth with a red paper napkin with Santa Claus's face in the center. "It's not that and you know it, Hal. You know I trust you, and I believe in your visions. I guess it's just my sense of duty, and the possibility I could tell you something and you'll pursue it, then get hurt. Then *I* won't be able to live with myself."

I grabbed his hand and tightened my grip. "Then let's make a deal. I swear on our friendship if I come across something that needs investigating, I'll tell you. I won't make a move without you. Girl Scout's honor."

His lips went thin, his eyes skeptical. "You weren't a Girl Scout, Hal."

I rolled my eyes. "Right you are. But I was a Brownie. Is there really a difference?"

He gave me a lopsided grin. "For like twelve

seconds, until Peggy Pullman made you mad and you turned her lunch into a—" He stopped short, remembering Hobbs was there.

"Pile of worms," I finished, wincing. Yeah. That had been an abysmally bad day. "Overreaction…"

"Uh, ya think?"

"I didn't mean to turn her sandwich into worms. I meant to turn it into spinach. Peggy Pullman hated spinach," I explained. "But in my defense, she was really mean, Stiles. She tied those stupid knots we were learning at Brownie camp with my shoe laces. I fell and whacked up my face pretty good, remember? Busted up my nose and split my lip."

Hobbs finally burst out laughing as he nudged me. "Worms?"

"Wait!" Stiles almost shouted when he realized we were talking about my magic out in the open. He leaned into me, talking out of the side of his mouth as he thumbed his finger at Hobbs. "Dainty knows…about?"

"Oh! I forgot to tell you. I told Hobbs everything last night."

"*Everything?*" Stiles squeaked, his eyes wide.

"Everything," I confirmed with a nod and a smile.

"And this happened after your last crime-solving caper where you nearly gave me a heart attack?"

I grinned at him. "Yes, Stiles. After that."

He looked at Hobbs and tipped an imaginary hat to him. "Well, you didn't run off to parts unknown, so I guess you're taking this okay?"

Hobbs winked. "I won't say she didn't knock me for a loop."

"Didja ask stupid questions?"

Hobbs cocked an eyebrow. "Like?"

"Like, does she ride a broom," Stiles cackled.

Hobbs gave us a sheepish glance. "I mean, c'mon, man. When you found out, wasn't that the first thing you wondered?"

Stiles barked a laugh. "When I could actually speak again, that *was* my very first question. Remember that, Hal?"

Now I laughed. "I sure do. What is it with you two and your obsession with brooms?"

"Aw, c'mon, honey," Hobbs said in protest, wrapping an arm around me. "I think it's a fair question. I mean, who didn't grow up watching *Bewitched*? Right, Stiles?"

Stiles stuck his square jaw out at me. "Yeah. What Dainty said. See? You made fun of me, too, but that was the first thing that came to mind. You riding on a broom in a silhouette across the moon."

"That's a TV show, you knuckleheads, and no witch I know wiggles her nose to cast a spell," I whispered with a scoff, looking around to see if we'd drawn any attention.

Stiles rolled his eyes. "Whatever. Either way, I'm glad you know, buddy, and you didn't head for the hills, or I'd have to hunt you down for hurting my BFF."

My heart warmed. Stiles always looked out for me. "Okay, all the protective big brother stuff aside, will you let me help with the investigation? Let *us* help?

People are more likely to let their guards down and talk to a couple of nobodies than they are the police. Think of it that way."

Stiles took the last bite of his egg salad sandwich and popped a chip in his mouth, crunching on it as he quite obviously pondered.

"If you don't want me to hear anything, I can hit the bricks, bud," Hobbs offered.

Stiles wiped his mouth. "Nah. It's fine. As long as you both promise to keep your mouths shut, I'll tell you what I know. But you have to swear to me you'll be careful, Hal. Swear it."

"You wanna do a blood oath?" I asked with a smug grin. He'd made me do it once when he made me swear I wouldn't tell Zeke Barns that Stiles was in love with him.

When we pricked our fingers with sewing needles to seal our deal, Stiles gagged and almost passed out. Stiles wasn't great with the sight of blood—which always made his profession choice a curious one to me.

He wrinkled his nose and shook his head. "That's gross."

"Baby," I taunted like the days of old.

"I was ten, Hal."

I stuck my tongue out at him and stole a chip from his plate with a facetious grin. "So was I."

Hobbs rolled his eyes. "Okay, you guys. Y'all stop whizzin' on each other's trees and let's make a deal so we can figure out what goin' on with this woman Hal saw in her vision."

We both straightened at that and tried to keep serious faces, but Stiles nudged me with his feet under the table, making us both fight to keep from laughing.

"Knock it off!" I whisper-yelled at him, widening my eyes. "I promise, okay. I swear it on my favorite throw pillows. I promise I'll be careful and not take any unnecessary risks. I didn't mean to take the ones I took in the first place. They just happened."

But Stiles reminded me, "You didn't just *happen* to follow that car to the last murder, Kitten. That was a risk you meant to take. It was no accident."

A minor case of guilt washed over me. "Okay, so I was impulsive. But I had to do something."

"The something you should have done was call the police, not follow a suspect. I'm not saying this to be a jerkface, Hal. I'm saying this because I love you. You're my best friend, and I'd probably curl up in a ball and die in a corner if you were hurt."

I rolled my eyes at him and tapped his hand. "You're being dramatic and you know it."

He grinned at me, his white, even teeth flashing his familiar smile. "Maybe a little. Curling up in a ball is dramatic, but I definitely wouldn't eat for a little while."

"Oooo. No food? You really would miss me," I teased, hoping to lighten the darkening mood.

Then my best friend sobered. "I really would."

"If I promise not to do it again, will you let me help?"

"Swear it," he demanded again.

I raised my right hand and put my left one over my heart. "I swear on the BFF code."

He held out his pinky and I linked mine with his to seal the deal. "Thank you. Now, here's what I know. Joey Scarpetti isn't Joey Scarpetti from Madison, Wisconsin, but we have no idea *who* he is—yet. No fingerprints in the system, meaning he wasn't wanted for anything illegal. We've got a forensic dentist checking his teeth to try and figure out who this kid is. Also nothing yet on hair or skin samples. Until then, we don't have a lot."

Hobbs gave Stiles a strange look. "Did you talk to Saul about his work application? I mean, how did Joey get the job without a social security card and all the stuff you need to apply?"

"All of it was fake," Stiles supplied with a cluck of his tongue.

"How did Saul miss that?" I asked. Saul was usually so meticulous about background checks and refer-ences. For that matter, he was always careful about the personalities he hired—meaning, they had to fit with his team.

"I don't know, and Saul says *he* doesn't know how he missed it either, but he did, and we have a dead kid on our hands with no identity."

I cupped my chin and thought about that. "It feels like he came here with an intention of some kind. He kept a low profile, no trouble. No drama. Kept his head down. Maybe the person who killed him did something to him, and he was here to get revenge and it all went kerflooey?"

Stiles stuffed his notepad back in his pocket. "Maybe. Or maybe he was just in the wrong place at the wrong time, but it's too early to speculate at this point with no background info. Everything else is a projection."

I couldn't help but scoff. "Did you see my pear tree, Stiles? That doesn't feel like wrong place, wrong time. Someone really hacked it up, and they really hacked poor Joey up. That felt like rage, not wrong place, wrong time."

"Yeah, I'll give you that. It sure looked like rage," Stiles agreed.

I bit my lip. "Cause of death? Or is it too early to determine? I mean, from what I saw, he had some holes in him, but he didn't die from falling off the lift, right? He was stabbed with something."

"Prelim investigations says a puncture wound to the carotid is what did it, and he was definitely dead when he fell from the lift. Probably happened sometime in the very early hours of the morning before the sun was up."

"So it happened this morning?" I asked, incredulous. I'd tossed and turned all dang night, for goodness sake. "How did I miss that, Stiles? How did Atti and Nana? I mean, a fight like that had to at least make some noise, right?"

"How did I?" Hobbs said. "I was up late last night."

"How late?" Stiles asked.

Hobbs let his palm drop to the table. "My head-phones! I was listenin' to some Garth. Must have happened when I had 'Friends in Low Places' up loud. I guess it was about two or three in the morning."

I nudged Hobbs in the ribs. "You listen to Garth Brooks?"

His response? "It's therapeutic. Relaxes me, and Garth and I are old friends."

Why did Hobbs need therapeutic music?

Stiles tapped his finger on the Formica table. "Is the man's playlist the point here, Hal?"

I put my serious face back on and refocused my thoughts. "Sorry. I don't know how I missed something that…messy. Or that eventful."

"It definitely was messy and the evidence says whoever put Scarpetti on the lift was no dummy and absolutely not a weakling."

Hobbs's eyebrows rose in question. "How so?"

Stiles pulled out his notepad again and flipped the pages. "They had to drag him at least a quarter mile from Hal's property to the nearest lift entry. We found some tree remnants that left sort of a bread crumb trail partway to the lifts, but no good footprints or anything because of the snowfall. Still, Joey was a hundred and sixty-five pounds and five-ten. Not an easy package to carry, especially if it's a limp one and in such deep snow."

"So we're looking for a big guy? Or maybe he used a sled? Something to carry the body with?" I suggested. It wouldn't be the first time a sled was used in a murder.

"Maybe, but the murder weapon says that's a lot to clean up and carry."

My spine tingled and my hands clenched. Something had sure hacked up that pear tree, and someone had put up a heck of a fight to avoid it.

"What was the murder weapon?"

"A ski pole."

"*a* ski pole?" My immediate thoughts went to Troy...

"Yep. They're pretty sharp in order to grab the snow. So if the perp had skis and ski poles, and a dead body, a sled feels like a lot to add to the mix."

"But *the perp*," I reminded (I couldn't believe I was using police jargon like some wannabe cop), "could have gone back to the lodge, dropped all those things off, gotten a sled and put Joey in it to drag him back to the lifts, right? It was early enough in the morning that he or she would have had time. Most everyone was still asleep. The likelihood someone would see them was very slim."

"Also true, and a good point, Officer Valentine," Stiles teased. "Forensics is trying to identify the brand of pole, and of course, there's a lockdown on all of Saul's rentals right now, which is what has people so upset with us. We're ruining their vacation because someone had the nerve to die and we're trying to catch a killer."

I exhaled a ragged breath. "Sorry, friend. People can be selfish sometimes." No one wants to have a murder in the middle of their Christmas vacation, but leapin' lizards, cut the police a break. "Did you search Joey's room in the bunkhouse?"

"We did, and came up dry. He's rooming with a guy named Marcelle Perdue. Nice kid from New York, who says Joey was there before he went to sleep at midnight. They sat up and shot the breeze about nothing for a half hour or so. Marcelle went to bed because he had an early shift, and when he woke up at six this morning, his bed was made and Joey was already gone."

Because by then he was dead.

I gulped, tucking my hands into the pocket of my hoodie and rocking back on my chair. "Do you mind if we talk to Marcelle?"

Stiles scratched his head. "I don't, but keep it on the down low. Ansel's not going to like it if he finds out you're in the middle of a murder again."

"Is he afraid my girl'll make y'all look bad?" Hobbs joked with a hearty chuckle.

Stiles laughed, too. "I think he is."

But I exhaled another breath in aggravation. I had an advantage I couldn't share and no one would believe me if I did, anyway. Regardless, I had one, and I was going to use it for good.

The whole puffed-out-chest thing on the PD's part

was such nonsense, I had to ignore it for the moment. "The goal is to find a killer. Not make people look bad, gentlemen. I'm not trying to steal anyone's shine, but I'm not going to stop until I find out who the girl in my vision is. She's connected to Joey, or whoever he is, and she's going to hurt herself if I don't figure it out."

I knew my tone had taken on a desperate quality, but I *was* desperate. If the girl was still alive, I was going to do whatever I could to prevent her from leaving this world.

And if she wasn't? If this had already happened?

I don't know what I'll do.

Stiles shot me a sympathetic smile. "I know, Kitten. I get it. You're in a crappy spot. One I don't envy."

"Have you talked to Troy? I don't think he could be a suspect, because he looked like he'd just seen someone rise from the dead when we first saw the pear tree, but he could be a really good actor, too."

"He has an alibi," Stiles assured me. "He was with a young lady by the name of Trina Downs from Vermont. They were together all night in one of the ski huts." The ski huts were small, heated little houses where you could stop along the cross-country ski hill if you needed to rest or grab a water.

Boy, did I remember the ski huts and all the hanky-panky that went on in them when I was in high school and we all went night tubing.

"Everything old is new again, huh?" I responded on a grin.

Stiles snorted at the memory. "Some things never

change. Anyway, she vouches for him and he did the same for her."

"They didn't hear anything either, I suppose?" Hobbs asked, his question tinged with amused sarcasm.

Stiles nodded his dark head in agreement. "Not a peep. But to be fair, the hut they were in was pretty far away from the crime scene."

As relieved as I was to hear Troy was in the clear, for his sake as well as Saul's, that left us with no one. How do you find out about a guy who was quiet, hardly ever talked to anyone, and didn't really exist anyway?

I told Stiles what Clarissa had told me about the head housekeeper's encounter with Joey, and he put Millie on his list of people to speak with.

Stiles pushed off from the table. "Okay, kids, I have to hit it. Do me a favor, Hal?"

I rose from my chair as well, coming around the table to give him a quick hug before patting his broad chest. "Anything."

He dropped a kiss on my forehead. "Stay out of the line of fire, okay? Don't get caught talking to people—especially by Ansel—and don't let the cat out of the bag, and most of all, don't get hurt."

"Promise," I assured him.

He pulled his jacket on and said over his shoulder, "Watch my girl, Dainty. Keep her on the straight and narrow."

"As if," Hobbs muttered under his breath. But he called back out to Stiles, "You bet, buddy."

I swatted his arm as Stiles strode out the door. "Whadda ya mean, 'as if'?"

Hobbs touched his nose to mine, his minty breath wafting over my cheeks. "Who was the last person who kept you on the straight and narrow, Cowgirl?"

"Um, I can only tell you what happened to the last person who *tried* to keep me on the straight and narrow."

"What happened to them?"

I clasped my hands behind my back and gave him an impish grin. "He had a bad case of bed bugs. Quite sudden, I hear."

Hobbs grinned and pressed a kiss to my nose. "Exactly. Now c'mon, Crockett, let's do this."

I put my hands on my hips. "I assume you're playing the role of the brooding yet smartly dressed Tubbs?"

He winked. "Yep. That'd be me."

"Why do I have to wear all the ice-cream-colored suits and loafers with no socks?"

"Because you're better lookin'."

I giggled. "Acceptable answer, Tubbs."

"Now c'mon. We're gonna find us a killer and save a girl. *I can feel it comin' in the air tonight,*" he sang with his dulcet Southern tones.

I laughed and sent out a silent prayer to the universe that was true. I took his hand as we left to go find some more people to question with the hope we'd be able to at least discover the name of the woman in my vision.

"I wish I could tell you something that would help," said Marcelle, Joey's roommate, who worked in the lodge's ski shop.

I looked down at the note Marcelle showed us from Joey—one he'd remembered after the police questioned him. Though the note didn't say anything that appeared to do with his death.

It was nothing more than a yellow sticky note reminder Joey had stuck to the fridge for Marcelle, so he'd remember to take his diabetes medication every morning when he woke up. But Marcelle had forgotten all about it after the chaos of finding out Joey was dead.

Joey wasn't only a nice guy with a fake name and place of residence, he was kind and he looked out for others.

I'd taken a picture of it and told Marcelle to give it to the police. I didn't know if Joey's handwriting might come into play, but every bit of evidence could only help.

"Hey, thanks, Marcelle. Appreciate you takin' the time to talk to us and for being so open," Hobbs said, holding out his hand to the slight boy.

Marcelle nodded his dark, curly head and shook Hobbs's hand. "Thank you, sir. I sure hope you find whoever did this. It's got us all pretty freaked. Joey didn't deserve to die like that. He was a great guy. He did nice stuff for everyone all the time in the short time he was here—like the reminder note about my diabetes

—and he was a great roommate." He pushed his thick glasses back up his nose and turned to head toward the lodge.

Again with the nice-guy schtick. Who wanted to kill such a nice guy?

But Marcelle maintained Joey was easygoing, neat and helpful. Which is what two of his fellow waiters had said, before we got to Marcelle.

No one else had ever heard him on the phone talking to anyone, and he never talked about where he came from or his family.

With a ragged sigh, I looked to Hobbs as we stood outside the festively decorated barn that served as a bunkhouse for the lodge employees and tucked my chin into my thick scarf, discouraged and cold.

Glancing up at the sky preparing to dump more snow on us, I wondered out loud, "So who wants to kill a nice guy, Tubbs?"

My handsome boyfriend clucked his tongue and shrugged. "I dunno, Crockett, but I don't think it was Marcelle who did it."

"That's a quick assumption. Why do you say that?"

"Does he look like he could carry a dead body a quarter mile?"

Marcelle was, in fact, slight of build, but that didn't leave him out of the suspect pool. "You'd be surprised what adrenaline can do, and I think if you've just killed someone, and you don't want to get caught, your adrenaline would be pumping and you could probably lift a Redwood if it means saving your skin."

Hobbs jabbed the air with his finger. "Good point, but you gotta admit, he's doubtful."

"I admit he's a longshot, but stranger things have happened."

"If that's not the understatement of the year," he teased. "So where to next, Crockett? You wanna cruise the beach and pick up chicks? Grab a fruity drink with an umbrella at the local tiki hut? Or should we talk to more people in an aimless circle of questioning?"

"What you're saying is we're going nowhere fast, right?"

Hobbs put a hand on my shoulder and nodded somberly. "I think we need to regroup, honey. Make a better plan. One with clearer direction."

Yet, my heart skipped a beat. We didn't have time to waste. I pressed my forehead to his chest. "But if we stop to regroup, we could waste valuable time."

"And we could waste it asking the wrong people questions."

"Also a good point. I call we talk to Saul next. I left him a voicemail, but he hasn't gotten back to me, so how about we storm the castle and find him?"

Hobbs hitched his jaw toward the lodge and the tall windows in the lobby, where the twinkling Christmas lights around the frames had just turned on. "Well, by the looks of the inside of the lodge, he's got a lot of grumpy people who have a lot of time on their hands to complain. He's probably spinning in circles, trying to keep them all happy."

I threw my hands up, my nose beginning to run

from the cold. "So what next?" My fears were beginning to well up inside me, and frustration reared its ugly head.

"We get some hot chocolate from Gracie and take a breath."

I let my head fall back on my shoulders, trying to relax the tension in my neck. "You just want marshmallows."

He smiled in that placating way he had when he wanted something, but was using it to pretend it was for my own good. "I don't deny I love marshmallows, but I also want you to take a breather so we can go over what we have so far."

My heart sank to my stomach. "Which is nothing. It seems like that's all we ever have when a murder happens. Zip."

He held out his hand to pull me toward the parking lot. "That's not true, honey. We have stuff."

I stopped short, my boots kicking up snow as I caught sight of one of the ski huts. "Wait. Didn't Marcelle say Joey liked to go to the ski huts?"

"Yeah, he said he was trying to learn how to cross-country ski but he got tired really easily, which is common when you're learning, so he stopped at a hut."

"But he said he always stopped at one particular hut, and never varied from that one particular spot."

"Maybe that was the hut where his legs always gave out. You know, like a runner gets to a point in a race and they have to rally or stop?"

"Do these thighs say I know anything about running? But I don't think it would hurt to look inside the hut. Maybe he left something there, or maybe I'll have another vision with another clue—which, by the way, Universe," I said, looking up to the cloudy sky, "would be a really nice gesture on your behalf. I'd like a big, fat, juicy clue, please."

"Fine. But are we gonna do this before we get hot chocolate with marshmallows, Crockett?" he mock-whined with a stomp of his foot.

I tugged him along behind me as I prepared to climb the big hill. "We are, Tubbs."

His shoulders dropped and he comically moaned. "And on top of the delay on my hot chocolate with marshmallows, we're going to walk?"

"We are. Unless you want me to try and zap us up there?"

He gasped. "You can do that?"

"It was a joke, but yep, I can. Though, like I said last night, my magic is fluky sometimes. The last time I tried to zap myself somewhere, I ended up in Istanbul. I *think* it was Istanbul. I dunno. I just know it was somewhere really hot. I do remember that."

Hobbs gasped again, and this time he wasn't joking. I know that for sure, because his beautiful blue eyes grew round as saucers. *"Really?"*

"Yeah. Really."

"You've been to Istanbul?" he asked, his voice going squeaky with disbelief, making me laugh.

I made a face. "You'd think the idea I zapped myself

somewhere far, far away would hold more appeal than the actual location."

"But it's Istanbul," he said, his voice ringing with excitement. "I mean, how cool is that?"

I made a face. "It's not nearly as exciting as it sounds. It's hot and sticky and what I'm really trying to stress here is, my magic can be unpredictable—especially when I'm tense. That should be your takeaway. You don't want to end up in the outer regions of Nowhereland, do you?"

But he wasn't listening. "Can you zap us to Aruba?"

"Are you listening to me? When we figure this out, we're gonna have a long talk about what my magic can be used for. Until then, I'm going to zap you to Siberia with nothing but a pair of shorts and T-shirt if you don't knock it off, buddy. Now, c'mon, it's getting dark."

Gosh, I sounded like Atti, lecturing Hobbs on the pitfalls of using my magic for personal gain.

I dragged Hobbs up the hill toward the huts, sitting among the white landscape of empty hills. I loved sunset when the snow was on the ground and the pine trees hugged you close with their ice-dipped limbs.

The sky, bruised purple and white, hung low over our heads. So low, it felt like you could reach up and poke a puffy cloud. The ocean crashed in the distance and seagulls flew overhead, and in this moment, I couldn't imagine ever living anywhere else.

I loved New York and my time there, but nothing beat Marshmallow Hollow.

By the time we reached the top and counted out four huts from the left, the number of huts Marcelle said to count to get to Joey's favorite one, we were both breathless.

Maybe breathless is the wrong word. Gasping for air is probably a better picture. Regardless, I couldn't walk another inch, my legs felt like soft butter and, once more, I chastised myself for being in such bad shape. I flopped down on the snow. I didn't even care that I was going to get my jeans all wet.

"Why did we walk this again instead of taking a lift?" Hobbs asked as he flopped down next to me.

"Good cardio, and the lifts aren't running anyway," I managed to huff, sitting up on my elbows, only to sink farther into the deep snow.

He blew out a breath, a puff of condensation coming from his lips. "It's cold."

"And the sun's going down. What time is it anyway?"

It had to be close to four in the afternoon. Maine winter nights start early and get colder as they go.

He pulled his phone from his jacket pocket and sat up. "Almost four. Sun sets so early these days. We'd better get in and get out before it gets too dark."

I pushed myself off the ground with great reluctance. "Let's get 'er done so we can get you some hot chocolate and marshmallows, Cowboy."

We finished the last couple of hundred feet to the hut with raspy gasps for air. Hobbs reached for the handle of the quaint hut, resembling a tiny one-room chalet with its A-frame roof, white cedar shingles, and red door with a bedraggled Christmas wreath tacked on its surface.

As he went to pull it open, the door swung wide with such force, taking us both by such surprise, it knocked him back into me with a dull thud.

We both crashed to the ground, the hard-packed snow doing anything but softening the blow.

"Hey!" I yelped, as Hobbs's enormous body slammed on top of mine in a crunch of ski jackets and tangled limbs.

As we scrambled to pick ourselves up, I got a quick glimpse of someone running away, carrying something under their arm as though it was a football, sprinting into the thicket of trees surrounding the hill.

Hobbs was up and on his feet in surprisingly quick time, chasing after the person who'd just barreled into us. He thundered through the deep snow after whoever it was, yelling for them to stop.

I began to get nervous when things suddenly went quiet and I couldn't hear Hobbs's boots pounding the snow anymore.

"Hobbs? Hobbs, you okay?" I yelled out, my heart racing.

He burst out of the trees with a grunt and something in his hand.

I did the best I could to get to him as fast as my legs would let me, cursing the lack of exercise in my life as my thigh muscles burned and begged for me to stop.

When I managed to make it to him, his breaths came raggedly. "You okay?"

"I'm fine. It just knocked the wind out of me. How 'bout you? You okay?"

"Need—to—exercise—more—" he gasped, holding out an item to me.

I squinted at it in the waning daylight. "What is this…?"

Hobbs put his hands on his knees as I took the item from him. Panting and wheezing for air, he said, "He dropped it."

I held it up. It was an ornament.

A purple Christmas ornament.

CHAPTER 9

"*D*id you get a look at him?"

Hobbs shook his head as we headed back down the hill after he'd caught his breath. "I got a look at the *back* of him just as he dropped the ornament and shot off into the woods. He was in a dark hoodie—average height, average size, black ski boots—and it looked like he was carrying a box of some kind. But that's it. He was like a lightning bolt. I, on the other hand, was not. Too much butt in chair these days."

I paused for a second. Where had I heard that phrase about butts before? I was sure it referred to something other than exercise, but I couldn't remember what.

"What's wrong?"

I decided now wasn't the time to complicate things. I had to stick to the task at hand. "Nothing. Back to the guy who just knocked us down. You do think it was a man, don't you?"

"I do. Not a weak man, either. He burst out of that door like he was the Hulk. Knocked me over like I don't weigh two hundred and twenty-eight pounds."

I patted his flat belly. "Of solid muscle, Big Boy."

He laughed. "Of too many marshmallows and Christmas goodies. Anyway, he knocked me over like I was some lightweight, and we both know I'm not. Strong. Whoever he was, he was very strong."

"I put in a call to Stiles. Maybe they can get footprints or something from the impressions of his boots in the snow?"

"But what would they match them to? There were no footprints last night. Just a hacked-up tree and a torn, bloody shirt."

As we reached the bottom of the hill, I remembered the shirt. "Speaking of shirts, I wonder if they've gotten DNA or something from it yet? Surely the killer left something behind. Hair, skin, maybe? And off the trunk of the tree. There was hair there, too."

Hobbs nodded. "Maybe. I wanna know what he was looking for in the hut. Why was whatever he had so important? Why would he want to get his hands on the ornament?"

I held it up, trying not to touch it too much in case any fingerprints could be pulled from it, and looked at it in the rapidly deteriorating daylight. It wasn't anything special. A round, thread-wrapped ball in deep purple with a white glittery bow. I didn't doubt it was for whoever Sabrina was, but who was she, where was she…and what did she want Joey to erase?

"I think the bigger question is, why was Joey keeping things in the hut? It's obvious he used it as a hiding place, judging by the floorboards the thug pulled up to get to that box."

We'd done a quick search of the hut and it wasn't anything special. There was a small table with a battery-operated Santa who danced in the center, a small fridge with water and a chair.

But the floorboards in the corner had clearly been pried upward. Yet, there was nothing under them but a hole where the box had obviously been wedged.

Hobbs rubbed his hands together as we hit the front of the lodge. "Maybe he was afraid to keep it in his room? It's tight quarters in the bunkhouse. Maybe he was worried someone would find it."

"But what's in that box? What didn't he want anyone to find? Was it even Joey's box to begin with? Maybe it's just a box with a purple ornament."

"Which just happens to be the woman in your vision's favorite color. Not to mention, Joey promised Sabrina a purple ornament. And lastly, who runs away like that if they're not doing something suspish?" Hobbs pointed out.

My little town was falling apart at the seams these days and it made me stop and wonder. "What the heck is going on in Marshmallow Hollow?"

He rubbed his temples. "The million-dollar question of the day. Look, I'm going to go grab the Jeep. It's almost dinnertime and we need to refuel. *I* need to refuel. Let's grab something to eat and go over what we have."

I nodded in agreement. I'd only had soup for lunch and it wasn't sticking with me very well. I was hungry, too. "Okay, but look," I said, pointing to the window, "there's Saul. While you grab the car, I'm going to hit him up with a couple of questions."

Hobbs planted a kiss on my lips. "Don't learn anything too interesting without me."

I saluted him. "Aye-aye, Cowboy. See you in a minute."

Making my way inside the lodge, letting the warmth of the big fireplace seep into my chilled bones, I waved to Saul, who looked harried and upset.

A fit, really good-looking man in brown slacks and a red polo shirt paced back and forth in front of the desk, and he looked pretty mad.

Approaching Saul, I put a hand on his arm. "What's going on, Saul?"

He held up what looked like a tiny nanny cam. "This!" he bellowed, his normally red face now cherry red. "My guest, Mr. Talbot here, found it in his bathroom!"

My mouth fell open. "Where exactly did he find it?"

"In the arrangement of fake poinsettias on the bathroom sink. His wife accidentally knocked it over and this fell out," Saul spat.

"I want my money, Sanderson, and you'd better believe whoever's on the other end of that camera's going to pay—big time. Count on it!" Mr.

Talbot virtually growled, his lean, handsome face red with anger.

So now, on top of everything else, the lodge had a peeping Tom?

What was happening?

Saul immediately began apologizing to Mr. Talbot, his Maine accent growing thicker. "My deepest apologies, Mr. Talbot, and to Mrs. Talbot, too. Of course I'll comp you the room and all your meals."

Poor Saul. He looked beside himself, and who wouldn't? First his employee is murdered during one of the busiest times of the year, and then a nanny cam is found in one of his rooms? Bad for business.

"You'd better, and I want another room, right now! I can't get a flight out of this godforsaken fairytale town until the end of the week, but I'm not staying in a room that reminds my wife she's been spied on!" Mr. Talbot shouted, the veins in his lean neck sticking out before he stomped off, his wide feet encased in shiny black shoes, his face a mask of fury.

"Oh, Saul," I sympathized. "How can I help?"

Leaning forward on the counter, he put his head in his hands. "I don't understand what's happening around here. First that poor kid Joey and now this. I gotta call the police and report it."

Saul was a great guy, he worked hard to make everyone's experience at the lodge a good one. My heart hurt for him. "Let's call Stiles and report this, yes? I'll do it."

"Thanks, kiddo. That'd be a big help. As you can see,

I got my hands full today." He spread his hands to show me the chaos of the lobby.

As I called Stiles, I asked, "Has anything like this ever happened before, Saul?"

He lifted his burly shoulders as he pulled off his Santa hat, letting it drop to the shiny countertop. "Not that I know of. Meaning, if someone put a camera in a room, no one's ever found one. It was just lucky that Mrs. Talbot accidentally knocked over that arrangement and we found it. Now I'm gonna have to sweep all the rooms."

His statement made me wonder a multitude of things. First, lots of mini-cams had WiFi these days, along with apps. Could we locate the mini-cam owner if we connected it to a WiFi user? Could that even be done?

Second, if the cam didn't have WiFi, didn't someone have to collect the camera to watch the footage? I didn't understand the logistics of something like that at all.

I had someone who dealt with the security of our website and cameras at Just Claus for that reason— because tech wasn't my specialty. It wasn't even a little something I understood. But I was going to research it and find out.

A chill raced up my spine at the thought that someone was getting their kicks watching unsuspecting people bathe.

I left a message for Stiles, but it wasn't necessary.

He came strolling into the lobby just as I was hanging up.

"Never a dull moment, huh, Kitten?" Stiles said, his face grim.

"I was just leaving you a message. It's like you read my mind."

"He read *mine*," Hobbs said, coming up behind Stiles. "I called to tell him about the incident at the ski hut."

Stiles's eyes were bleary with dark shadows under them. "Man, what the heck is happening in Marshmallow Hollow?" he asked me wearily.

I patted his arm. "I was just wondering the same thing. Listen, are you here to look into the thing that happened out on the hill?"

"Yep."

I hated to do it, because I felt as though I was piling on, but it had to be done. "Well, there's something else now, too."

I explained to both he and Hobbs about the camera in the Talbots' room.

With a ragged sigh, Stiles radioed back to the station to send more people out to help him so he could investigate the Talbots' room.

"Do you mind if I shadow you?" I asked in a whisper. "Maybe I can pick something up?"

He took hold of my arm and pulled me to a corner of the lobby. "Are you thinking Joey's murder is related to this?"

I shrugged, pulling off my jacket and draping it over

my arm. "I don't know, but even if it isn't, maybe I can catch at least one jerkface. That's something, right?"

"Right. Just keep a low profile. I don't know where Ansel is, and I don't need him on my back when I can't give him the real explanation."

"Lead the way."

"I'll be lookout," Hobbs offered. "If Ansel shows up, I'll text a 9-1-1."

I smiled at this handsome man who'd mostly accepted all the nutty things happening around him that had to do with my life without so much as a crossed eye.

I felt awful for thinking so many horrible things about whoever that woman was, having coffee with him. I was glad I hadn't rushed to judgement in the heat of the moment.

I gave him a kiss and patted his hard chest. "I like you, Tubbs. You're the best sidekick a girl could ever have."

"Sidekick, huh? Does that make you lead investigator?" he teased.

"Just for the moment. I'll hand off the magnifying glass and notepad when I come back. We'll take turns being the big dog."

He laughed. "Go get 'em, tiger."

I wagged my fingers over my shoulder and ran after Stiles, who was getting the key card from Saul.

We headed upstairs via the long staircase, following the swirling greenery with red bows tacked on it and twinkling lights draped along the walnut bannister.

We made our way down the hallway that led to the rooms, our footsteps hushed on the patterned carpet. Stopping at the wood-stained door where Mr. Talbot's wife had found the camera, my stomach began to revolt.

I'm not sure why, but nausea assaulted my gut and my throat clogged with bile. The visceral reaction was odd enough that even Stiles noticed.

"You okay, Kitten? You look kinda green around the gills."

Swallowing back the acrid taste in my throat, I nodded. "I'm good. Let's do this."

Before I hurl my insides on the floor.

But when he swung the door open, revealing the warmly decorated room with a four-poster bed, a cheerful red ticking quilt and a fluffy white marabou throw blanket at the end, my cheeks went hot.

I had to grab at the wall to keep from falling over on my face.

An overwhelming sense of doom, of despair, of complete humiliation crept into my heart, prickling along my skin until the emotions felt like entities crawling along my arms.

"Kitten?"

Taking deep breaths, I ignored Stiles without meaning to and forced myself to walk fully into the room, until I was at the end of the king-size bed.

My fingers reached out to touch the marabou throw, the soft, fuzzy material soothing me as I stroked it and stared at the headboard.

A vision of the burgundy-haired woman flashed before my eyes. I heard her laughter. I was consumed with the remembered sound of her cries, now embedded in my ears.

Stiles put his hands on my shoulders. "Hal? Honey? You okay? What's happening?"

I blinked, realizing tears were falling down my face. Swiping at them, I shook my head. "Nothing's okay," I mumbled.

He physically turned me around. "What?"

I couldn't explain the sense of helplessness I felt, the notion that it was too much effort to take another breath, but the words, "Bad things happened in this room," fell out of my mouth before I could stop them.

CHAPTER 10

Stiles's face came into my line of vision as I came back from wherever I'd been.

"Kitten? You okay? Did you have a vision?"

I shook free of the image in my head, pressing a hand to my temple as though it would wipe away the picture of the woman with the burgundy hair.

"I don't think it was a vision. It was more like a...a memory. I could still move, something I can't do when I have a vision. But it was the awful feeling that came with it. Like, I couldn't go on another single second if I didn't get away from this bad thing that's chasing me."

Stiles handsome face came into focus. "What was chasing you?"

A helpless feeling of dread washed over me. "That's the thing, Stiles. I don't know. The only thing I know for sure is the woman in my vision's been here—or near here. I know it. We need to find out the names of every single person who's stayed in the rooms on this floor over the last year or so. Maybe longer. Something happened here, and if I were to make a speculation, it has to do with that nanny cam. Who knows how long it's been here and what it saw, but ask yourself this: what do people use hidden nanny cams for? It's not always to catch the nanny in the act of something horrible."

Stiles blanched, his ruddy face going pale. "So you think maybe the person who's responsible for the nanny cam was videoing women changing?"

"Or engaging in behind-closed-door activities..." I swallowed hard after saying those words out loud.

Stiles stayed silent for a second, both of us absorbing that information.

Gripping my hand, he squeezed it. "You're right. So do we think the woman in your vision was here in one of the rooms, and someone used that hidden camera to try to exploit her? It happens all the time. I read about a case the other day where this guy stalked people for years and years on the Internet and got away with it, because there were really no definitive cyber laws against what he was doing."

I scrubbed my eyes and forced myself to try to remember something else from my vision, but to no avail. "But there are laws about videoing someone without their knowledge. I think for sure the woman in my vision has something to do with it. I don't know what happened here, but if this is about her, if this room is connected to her, it was bad enough that she'd want to end her life—if she hasn't already."

Stiles stiffened before he let go of my hand. "I'd better get to searching the rooms. You wanna stay or have you had enough?"

"My gut says you won't find anything else. I'd definitely do a sweep of the room for fingerprints and all that good forensic stuff, but I don't think you're going to find anything else of significance."

"Crud," Stiles muttered.

That feeling of dread began to seep deeper into my bones, the feeling of urgency I couldn't shake, and that meant I needed to figure this out—and soon.

But I had to get out of this room. It made my stomach hurt. "I'm outta here. I'll text you if I find out anything. Have you talked to Clarissa yet? Or Millie?"

"There are two other guys who've been questioning them. If I get anything of significance, I'll text you."

"Ditto," I called over my shoulder as I hurried out of the room and into the hallway.

I practically ran down the stairs to get out of the vicinity of that room and fell straight into Hobbs's arms at the end of the staircase.

"Whoa there, Crockett. What happened?"

"Come with me." I pushed him away from the stairs and back toward the lobby—away from the bad feeling I hadn't been able to shake. "I'll tell you over dinner. You wanna have something delivered? I don't want to have to worry about people overhearing us, and I need to be somewhere that makes me feel good."

He smiled at me, wrapping his arms around my waist and giving me a warm hug. "Sounds good to me."

Over Hobbs's shoulder, I happened to see Abel Ackerman, zipping through the center of the lobby as though he was being chased by the hounds of Hell. "There's Abel. Let's catch him and see if he knows anything about Joey before he runs off to put out another fire."

"Abel!" Hobbs called out with a sharp whistle.

He turned at the call of his name and frowned, but I stepped out of Hobbs's hulking shadow and waved him over, and he smiled.

As he approached us, he tucked his clipboard under his armpit, his steps crisp and made with precision as he dodged guests preparing for dinner.

I greeted him with a warm smile. "Abel. How are you? I mean, under the circumstances."

His lean face screwed up into a look of distaste. "Well, if you consider there's been a murder, and now I hear a webcam was found in the Talbots' room, which I suppose means we have a peeping Tom? So on a scale of one to ten, I'm gonna give today a big fat minus zero."

Laughing, I nodded. If I didn't laugh, I'd cry. Abel was a nice enough guy. He'd been at the lodge for about a year, taking over guest services when Sally Longworth had left to go off to Hawaii for a guest services position with a big hotel on Honolulu.

I didn't know a lot about him, other than we'd seen each other from time to time at various establishments around Marshmallow Hollow, and he was always friendly and polite.

Though, Saul always spoke kindly of him, even if

he'd labeled him "anal." In his line of work, being detail-oriented had to be a benefit.

He came from Idaho, after doing a cruise ship stint. In his late twenties, he was nice, direct, and most of all, clean-cut and easily relatable—another quality essential in dealing with guests.

"It's been a rough day for you, I'm sure, and now you have all these guests to contend with who can't do any of the activities they paid to do. This has to be a nightmare for you," I sympathized.

He sighed and nodded. "If you only knew." Then he straightened his spine as though to remind himself whining wouldn't get him anywhere. "So what can I do for you, Miss Valentine?"

"Just call me Hal, and I was wondering if you knew anything about Joey Scarpetti?"

He blinked and cocked his dark blond head. "Like? We didn't work in the same areas of the lodge. He was food service, I'm guest services. Though, to be real honest, today I almost wish I was in food service," he answered with a small, ironic laugh.

"Did you know him at all? It seems like no one really knew Joey. I know he wasn't here very long, but I was just trying to get some insight on him."

"Because you're Marshmallow Hollow's answer to Jessica Fletcher?" he asked, and I wasn't sure if he was being sarcastic or teasing me.

"Because Saul's my friend and I was hoping to help him out."

Abel put his head down and looked at his feet

before meeting my eyes. "Sorry. I didn't mean that to sound rude. It's just what everyone's saying about you and your cowboy."

Yeah, and it was starting to make me cranky. But I couldn't tell anyone why I was trying to help, now could I? Or even how I could help, for that matter. Still, I didn't love his tone, but I decided to ignore it in favor of any information I could get my hands on when it came to Joey Scarpetti.

"It's fine, Abel. Anyway, did you ever get a chance to talk to Joey? Hang out?"

He smiled again, almost in a fond way. "In passing, but mostly my job keeps me on the outskirts of the kitchen. We said hello and good morning, etcetera, etcetera. Just the usual pleasantries among co-workers, you know?"

"So nothing unusual? You never saw any arguments with anyone, nothing out of the ordinary?"

Abel ran a knuckle over his chin. "Nothing really unusual. He was a pretty nice guy for the most part, kept to himself."

I swear, if I heard Joey was a nice guy one more time... Who kills nice guys, and why? What did Joey know that got him killed?

"We've heard that from virtually everyone we've talked to since this afternoon," Hobbs remarked.

Abel paused for a moment, then he said, "Hang on. That's not entirely true. He wasn't always nice..." he eluded. "Maybe this is a stretch, when it comes to whether he was nice or not, but there was one time I heard him on his cell with someone, and I heard him say he had some stuff going on and he wasn't sure when he'd be back. I don't know what the other person said, but his face got really red at the response. It was probably the most emotion I've ever seen him show since he'd started at the lodge."

My alarm bells began to sing. "So he appeared angry?"

Abel scratched his head. "Angry, frustrated, something like that. Maybe he had a girlfriend back home in Wisconsin who wanted him to come back? I don't know."

That sick feeling, which had begun to dissipate, returned in my stomach. "When did this happen?"

"Just a few days ago. I remember because I was running around like a chicken with my head cut off, readying things for a group from the UK. They had a list of requests as long as my arm. What is a toad in the hole, anyway?" He shook his head and smiled. "Anyway, Joey was right outside the laundry room. I go there sometimes to get some peace and quiet, and he was in the hallway, on his cell. When he saw me, he held up a hand as though to apologize and walked off down the hall. And that was it."

Hobbs crossed his arms over his chest and I sensed skepticism in his next question. "And that's all you heard? Were those his exact words?"

"Yes, sir," he answered before he looked at his phone. "Listen, I'm swamped and I have to get back to my guests. We're having the scavenger hunt here

118

tonight instead of at the ice festival. Boy, did that take some rearranging with Clarissa. But that's okay. She's fun to work with. Anyway, I really gotta run. Anything else?"

I shook my head, mostly because my stomach was in knots. "No, Abel. That's all, but if you think of anything, take my number and give me a call. And make sure you tell the police what you told me."

He winked and wagged his fingers at us. "Already done. Bye, guys."

"He's a congenial guy, huh?" Hobbs commented.

"I feel like that statement has some subtext on the side."

Hobbs put his hand at my waist. "You could be right. He kinda rubs me the wrong way, and I don't know if it's his eternally sunshiney attitude or if it's just me."

"Well, he did time on a cruise ship. Isn't it mandatory that you have an eternally sunshiney attitude?"

"Fair enough. It definitely feels fake. But maybe the cruise ship thing is it."

"I'm not sure I agree, but I *can* tell you, I'm starving. Let's go home and order takeout."

As suddenly as Hobbs agreed, I heard Ansel calling my name. "Hal? Funny I should find you here," he quipped.

Without warning, Hobbs swept me up in his arms and planted a kiss on my lips, one so long and so earth-shattering, I forgot all about coming up with an explanation for Ansel.

"Oh, didn't mean to intrude," he muttered as he slipped past us and headed up the stairs, obviously heading to the Talbots' vacant room.

"Take me home, please?" I whispered against Hobbs's lips.

"Your chariot's right outside. C'mon, beautiful. Let's blow this joint and get you fed."

As Hobbs led me from the lodge, his strong hand gripping mine, the horrible feeling began to dissipate. As we drove back to the house, it eased completely.

But the fear of messing this up? That stayed with me.

***

We'd ordered Chinese and as I sat in front of the fire in the dining room, nibbling at my walnut shrimp, my favorite from Wu's, I was finally able to catch my breath.

"Halliday, I would have cooked for you both," Atti chastised as I swallowed some fried rice. He flew to the table and sat in front of my plate.

"Sometimes I just need some Wu's walnut shrimp, ya know? Anyway, distract me, tell me how your day was."

His feathers ruffled, the beautiful colors shimmering under the glow of Christmas lights. "Not nearly as dreadful as yours, I assure you. I narrowly escaped the black maw of Philistine, and Ms. Streisand finds the ornaments on the tree quite a grand time.

Stephen King, however, is as always the perfect gentleman."

Hobbs chuckled, seemingly unbothered by Atti talking to us, which meant he'd begun to accept and adjust. Or at least I hoped that was the case.

"Philistine." He repeated the nickname Atti had for Phil. "Funny."

"There's nothing I live for more than being your court jester," Atti assured him as he lifted off the table and flew to another part of the kitchen.

Hobbs laughed again. "Don't be sore, Atticus. Being funny is a compliment."

I chuckled, too. "Atti is nothing if not all business." Wiping my mouth, my stomach feeling better, along with my state of mind, I asked, "So, the scavenger hunt tonight. I got a text that confirms they've moved it inside the lodge. You still want to go?"

Hobbs reached across the table and gazed at me with his dreamy blue eyes. "I'm fine with goin'. The question is, how are you, and are *you* up to it?"

I'd told Hobbs what I'd experienced in the Talbots' room, and he was his usual understanding self. We'd considered asking to see the other rooms on the floor to see if I got the same feeling of dread, but it would only usurp the guests and make their stay more chaotic.

I had to leave that up to the police.

"I think if we don't, we might miss something. Plus, we still need to talk to Millie from housekeeping. I'm sure she'll be there because she has grandchildren."

Leaning back in his chair, Hobbs stretched his long arms. "Okay, so let's go over what we have and our possible suspects, so I can be up to speed. We have the victim, Joey, who's dead. Then there's Sabrina, who's somehow involved with Joey. Joey isn't really Joey but someone else entirely. Someone whose ID remains a mystery."

Nodding, I pulled my phone out and looked at the notes I'd jotted down throughout the day. "And Sierra heard him talk to Sabrina about a purple ornament and erasing something—a something we have no clue about."

Hobbs nodded, putting his napkin on his plate of finished food. "Also, there's Clarissa. She overheard Joey get upset with Millie, the head housekeeper— which we've heard a hundred times isn't like him— about the rooms, but we don't know what room or why he cared about it. He's obviously never been to the lodge before, or Saul would have mentioned knowing him before he became an employee."

A spark of a thought hit me square in my face. Something I hadn't put together until Hobbs mentioned the room and Millie. "So if we go by what we've learned so far, and Joey wanted to know who'd stayed in the lodge's rooms—where ironically, a webcam was found today—is it a stretch to think Joey knew about the webcam and either wanted to remove it or see what was on it? Maybe that's what he meant by erasing something? Maybe he's responsible for the webcam?"

"But if he's responsible for the webcam, why wouldn't he know what room it was in?"

I hopped up from the chair at the dining room table and began to pace because my legs wouldn't let me sit still. We were onto something. I felt it in my soul. "Maybe he wasn't responsible for putting it in the room. Maybe someone he loves, like *Sabrina*, is being exploited on that webcam and Joey came to find out who was doing it!"

Now Hobbs rose, too, making our resident pets stir in their beds by the fire. "A solid explanation. But why the mystery? Why did he sign up for a job at the lodge under a fake identity, just to find a webcam? Why wouldn't he just ask Sabrina what room she'd stayed in? And what difference does the room make, anyway? He couldn't have expected the webcam would still be there, could he? And lastly, why wouldn't he call the police and report it?"

That stopped me cold. "I don't know. And we *won't* know if we can't find out who he really is. Then we can potentially see if he's filed a police report. Though, the whole video cam thing is iffy when it comes to the law —or at least it was in that one episode I watched on Investigation ID. But the bigger question is, why would he take on the task himself? And is that what got him killed?"

"And we still don't have any solid suspects," Hobbs reminded me as he began clearing plates.

I joined him, grabbing our empty wine glasses to put in the dishwasher. "There's still Marcelle to consider. I know you doubt him as a possible suspect because he's smaller in stature, but stranger things have been known to happen."

Hobbs flipped on the tap and began rinsing dishes. "I do doubt he's a suspect. I definitely doubt he was whoever knocked us over tonight on the hill. That guy was no slouch."

I threw the towel over my shoulder and began to put away our leftovers. "You know what we haven't done? We haven't looked at any of the Facebook profiles for the people we've talked to today. And I have to look up Sabrina. I'll try under Scarpetti, but I think we both know it's a long shot at best. But that purple ornament was for her. I don't need any proof to tell me that. Now, we have to figure out how Joey and Sabrina are connected, and I really think it has to do with the webcam. Speaking of, we need to see the guest registry for the last year. Let me put that on my list of things to ask for from Saul."

As we quietly cleaned the kitchen together, I thought about the multitude of events that had happened over the course of the day, trying to string them all together to build a suspect, but no one really fit.

Every one of the people we talked to said Joey was a nice guy, with the exception of two circumstances where he'd appeared agitated, and neither instance involved the person who'd witnessed it.

Sighing, I grabbed the garbage from the trash can

and decided to take it out. Maybe the bitter cold air would help me see clearer.

"I'm gonna take the garbage out. Be right back," I muttered, heading to the mudroom to throw on my jacket.

As I trudged to the garbage bin, I kept going over and over the connection between Joey and Sabrina.

Was Sabrina the reason Joey was here and wanted to erase something? And what was on that dang webcam? It made perfect sense that he'd use the word "erase" if something unsavory were on it, yes. But how unsavory *was* unsavory?

The questions niggled me as I lifted the lid of the garbage to hurl the bag inside, only to catch sight of the trash Troy had gathered and thrown away for me this morning. I'd forgotten about it, but now in hindsight, those items could be important.

I pulled my phone out and hit the flashlight app in order to see better. That was when I saw the receipt and the discarded cup from the lodge's café, leaving me to wonder if maybe they belonged to Joey or the killer.

I couldn't say for sure how long they'd been there. I didn't notice the trampled trees until the day before, when I was getting out of the shower.

Throwing on my gloves in case they could be evidence, I scooped the items from the bin and brought them back inside.

Under the lights of the mudroom, I read the receipt. It was from a coffee place in Westbrook, Maine, called

Coffee is Life, and written on the front of the receipt was a name.

Grady.

Well, that could be anyone who was staying at the lodge. I'd have to check. I was about to take it inside to put it in a plastic bag for Stiles when the see-thru paper revealed something written on the back.

A website URL that looked like it was in Joey's handwriting. The message he'd left Marcelle was written in all caps except for the letter I in both diabetes and medication. Those were all in lowercase.

I flipped to the pic of the note for Marcelle and compared the two signatures. I was no expert, but they sure looked a lot alike, right down to the distinctive letter I in lowercase.

And again, that shiver of discovery sizzled along my spine.

Out of nothing more than curiosity, I typed the URL on the back of the receipt into my phone, not even considering I'd find anything of import.

Except, I found something all right.

Yikes, did I ever.

And all I can say is…bow-chick-a-wow-wow.

Cue canned, cheesy music.

e were back in Hobbs's Jeep on our way to the lodge to attend the scavenger hunt as I contemplated this website called Uncensored Intimacies, and I think you can guess what the star attraction was.

"So a porn site, huh?" Hobbs said as he turned into the parking lot of the lodge, his tires crunching over the snow. "Why do you suppose Joey—or is it Grady—was writing down porn websites?"

"Why anyone would write a website like that down on their receipt for a morning cup of Joe is beyond me. Is nothing sacred?"

He laughed as he pulled into a parking space. "I'm pretty sure even people who watch porn drink coffee, honey. But I'm not sure I'm making the connection. Despite the significant comparison in handwriting, everyone talked about how nice Joey was. Do nice guys watch porn?"

"I don't know, do they?" I retorted, giving him a saucy glance.

He laughed. "I won't say I haven't seen a thing or two. I was a teen once, too, but I promise if you scoured my computer, you'd find a lot of stuff, but porn wouldn't be one of them."

"That doesn't necessarily mean Joey isn't a nice guy, but you know what I think it is? I think it connects to him asking Millie about the room, which I'm betting an organ was the Talbots' room. And the webcam and telling Sabrina he'd make sure it got *erased*. We need to know who's stayed in that room, Hobbs. If a Sabrina did, we can connect her to Joey. For sure I can tell you from my gut, something bad happened there and the clock is ticking."

My stomach took a downward dive again at the thought that the woman in my vision was no longer with us. I *had* to figure this out.

Hobbs gripped the steering wheel and clucked his tongue. "Your theory is sound, Jessica Fletcher two-point-O. Basically, you think there's some incriminating video of this Sabrina from a room at the lodge. That makes the word erase he used on the phone make a lot more sense."

I patted his muscled thigh. "That's exactly what I think. Either that, or Joey's a total schmuck and he made an incriminating video of Sabrina—which makes zero sense, because I don't know about you, but I wouldn't want any ornament, purple or otherwise, from someone who'd taped me when I was nude or whatever. Anyway, either of those explanations might get you killed."

"But again, he used the word erase. He told Sabrina he'd find a way to erase it," Hobbs reminded me.

I looked at him under the dim lights of the radio, where soft Christmas music played, and agreed. "True. But maybe they're a couple and they're into that and it got into the wrong hands? I'm not sure why he'd end up dead over it. More than likely he was killed for trying to figure out who created the incriminating video. But is it of Sabrina or only someone else? More importantly, is she the woman with the burgundy hair in my visions? That's what we need to know."

He ran his finger down along my nose. "I love when your eyes light up with the fire of a good mystery. I say we get on it, Crockett. Now, you ready to win a gift certificate for the lodge spa?"

That was the grand prize for the scavenger hunt—a day of luxury at the lodge spa.

I held up my finger. "Wait one second. I want to look up this coffee place and send Stiles a text with what we found."

Hobbs pointed to his phone. "I looked up Sabrina Scarpetti and found three—one is a kid, and the other two are women in their sixties. Lots of Sabrinas, though. If you want to pick through profiles to see if anyone matches your vision."

I frowned. "Did you find anything on the Facebook profiles from our list of suspects?"

Hobbs's face looked grim. "Can we even call them

suspects? The pool is shallow, honey, but yes, I looked them all up and they all have Facebook pages—mostly private and with very few details. I learned that Abel likes to run marathons, and Marcelle enjoys a rousin' game of chess. Oh, and Clarissa, our perky events coordinator, likes Bruno Mars and Savannah Temple novels."

I snorted. Ugh. Savannah Temple. My BFFs favorite. "Well, there's no accounting for taste, I suppose, but hardly anything earth-shattering."

Landing on the coffee shop I'd searched for, I clicked on Coffee for Life in Westbrook, Maine, a town I wasn't terribly familiar with. Not a cheap place to live, according to Google.

"Another interesting, useless fact to note, none of our shallow pool of suspects are friends on Facebook. I cross referenced them all."

"Huh. How odd. Though, I can't say as I blame them. Think about all the trouble people get into by expressing their sometimes unpopular views on their Facebook pages. First, you have to face the people you work with, who might disagree. Second, people hunt them down and expose them and call their employers. They end up fired and bombarded by hate posts. I see it on Twitter all the time."

"I can definitely understand that. The Twitter phenom can be brutal."

Hobbs sounded as though he spoke from personal experience, but I didn't have time to pursue the subject.

My phone beeped a text then—one from Stiles that

made my mouth fall open. "It's Stiles. He says the murder weapon…you remember the ski pole, right? It wasn't from any of the poles rented at Saul's because none are missing or have any evidence of a crime. They're speculating someone brought one with them— if it was actually someone from the lodge who killed Joey…er, Grady. Still haven't uncovered his real identity, but I sent Stiles a text about what was in the trash and he's going to meet us here to collect what I found. And then something very interesting…"

"And that is?" Hobbs asked, his voice husky and low.

My fingers shook a little. "The webcam is attached to an app."

Hobbs turned to look at me. "Shut the front door! Who owns it?"

"They don't know. It's registered in—are you ready for this?—Macedonia…which is where the website is also listed."

"Meaning, they can't be prosecuted for the content because Macedonia has different laws?"

I blew out a breath and scrunched my eyes shut. "Yep."

"Well, dagnabbit."

Yeah. What he said.

The scavenger hunt was in full swing when we entered the lodge. Christmas music played, kids ran from place to place on the hunt and the adults, with cocktails in hand, laughed and searched for the list of clues we were given by none other than Clarissa, when we walked in.

She wore an elf's hat and a fun sweatshirt that read: There's No Business Like Snow Business. "No fair you're here, Miss Valentine!" she teased with a laugh, her cheerful face flushed. "You solve real crimes. This scavenger hunt should be a cakewalk for you."

I laughed along with her, mostly to humor her ridiculous statement. "No fear of that. I didn't really solve anything. I just fell into the answers. I'm sure someone much worthier than I am will win. We're just here for the night out and some eggnog."

She leaned into me then, her face suddenly serious. "Have you found out anything that'll help with who killed Joey?"

Sighing, I shook my head as I pulled off my knit hat, twisting the white material in my fingers. "No. Unfortunately, we haven't. See? I told you, I'm not really that good."

She patted me on the back in sympathy. "No worries. I'm sure the police will figure it out. Until then, go have fun and good luck!"

Talk about eternally sunshiney. Though, I suppose that was part of her job as much as it was Abel's.

"Thanks, Clarissa." I smiled in acknowledgment and took the list without really looking at it. My heart wasn't in a scavenger hunt. Not when I needed to find the woman in my vision and Joey's killer. Or was his name Grady? Dang, I sure wish the police would find out who Joey really is.

I stared at the list without really seeing it because I couldn't stop thinking about what might be on that webcam.

"Honey?" Hobbs said with a tap to the paper. "We doin' this?"

"I'd rather look and see if we can find Millie. Then I need to talk to Saul and see if he'll give me a guestlist of people who stayed in the rooms on that floor. Do you mind?"

"Does a coyote have forty-two teeth?"

I blinked up at my handsome man. "Um, I dunno. Do they?"

He held out the crook of his arm to me. "Yep. Just a silly bit of info I learned when I was doing some research."

"So that means yes?"

He chuckled. "That means yes."

"Then let's go find Saul."

He had to be around this madness somewhere. Saul never let an event go unattended. He was too concerned about his guests' well-being and comfort to miss it.

We slipped through the crowd of people, all looking appeased under the glow of the Christmas lights strung from corner to corner of the room. The big Christmas tree glowed brighter as folks milled around its silver and gold beauty.

In general, the spirits of the guests felt better tonight than they had this afternoon.

Sure as the day is long, I saw Saul over by the table where a spread of Christmas goodies sat buffet style. All sorts of cookies were displayed, and red and green popcorn balls, cakes, and confections lined the table, drawing Hobbs instantly.

"Evenin', Saul," he greeted him with a smile.

Saul's gruff face broke into a grin. "The cowboy, in the flesh! Help yourself, son. Plenty to eat for a big guy like you."

There was no stopping Hobbs when brownies were involved. "Don't mind if I do."

As Hobbs picked out some treats, I rested a hand on Saul's burly arm. "Hey, Saul? Can I trouble you for a sec of your time?"

"'Course you can, sweetheart. What can I do ya for?"

"First, how goes the room sweeps?"

His cheeks puffed as he blew out a breath. "Didn't find any more of those nasty things anywhere. The police made sure of that. Can't wait to see my Yelp reviews after this."

"Any idea at all who might have put it there?"

Saul sucked his teeth and shook his head. "Not a one, kiddo. I've never had anything like this happen before, but it makes my stomach roll like a ship on a stormy sea. Can't tell ya how upset I am about it, but the police say they can't find the owner of the dang thing because the ID something or other is in Macedonia. How's that gonna help me find who did this?"

"The IP," I provided. "It's like an Internet address, but the owner of the camera registered it in Macedonia so they can avoid prosecution."

Saul's round face went red. "'Cause they were doin' somethin' dirty with that camera, that's why!" Then he sighed. "All this is my fault, you know. If I did a better job of checking Joey's paperwork—or whatever the heck his real name is—he wouldn't be dead. I'll never forgive myself for that."

The remorse in his voice made my heart tighten. "Oh, Saul, I think he would have found a way. He was here for a reason. A man on a mission, so to speak. That's why I want to talk to you."

He smiled warmly at me, his eyes twinkling under the Christmas lights. "I've been hearin' how you helped with the other investigations. You just tell me what you need and I'm all in, kiddo. I don't care what the police say about it either."

I held my hands up in minimal protest. "I'd highly recommend you share anything you know with the police, Saul. I'm no mastermind sleuth. I just get a feeling every once in a while and I can't resist sticking my nose in. If I find anything, I'm going to share it. You should, too."

"If you say so, Hallie-Oop. I'll do what you ask. Now, what can I do ya for?"

"Would you happen to have the list of people who've stayed in the Talbots' room, and all the others on the same floor, over the last year or so? In fact, maybe the list of everyone who's stayed here in the last year?"

For all I knew, the webcam might have been moved around to different rooms without anyone being aware. Better to check them all.

"You got it, sweetheart," Saul said on a wink. "Gimme one sec and Loretta will print it out for you, but you gotta keep it confidential and all. I value my guests' privacy."

I smiled at him. "You can count on me. Also, any idea where I can find Millie? Is she here tonight?"

His expression became skeptical. "Millie Hart? She's here with the grandkids. Saw her not long ago. You're not tellin' me she's involved, are ya?"

"Oh no," I reassured him. "Not at all, but she did have an interaction with Joey I'd like to ask her about."

He scrubbed his hand over his face. "Man, I can't believe anyone would wanna hurt poor Joey. He was a nice kid, and even if he lied about who he is, he worked hard."

I fought a roll of my eyes. This guy had made quite an impression in such a short time. "So I've heard. But you never heard anything about him that might help figure out who he is? He didn't have any trouble with any of the other staff?"

Saul ran a beefy hand over his forehead. "Not a dang thing. He showed up on time for his shifts, sometimes he even got in early. He never complained. He was always pleasant to the guests, and he went above and beyond to do his job."

If Joey had any serious trouble with anyone it would make this too easy, wouldn't it? I needed a motive and so far, I had nothing.

I was beginning to think the person who'd killed Joey wasn't anyone at the lodge. The possibility that whoever owned that webcam was someone who wasn't even in the vicinity became more real than ever.

My next questions was a longshot, but worth a try regardless. "Do you remember a guest named Sabrina?"

Saul snorted at me. "Kiddo, I can barely remember *my* name. I only remember the regulars who come back year after year. But I don't remember a Sabrina."

Just as I'd thought. "Okay, Saul, let me know when you have the list printed and I'll go hunt for Millie."

"Deal," he said and handed me a brownie with a smile. "For your travels."

I grinned at him and grabbed Hobbs, who had brownie crumbs on his face I lovingly wiped away. "Good brownie?"

He grinned, a little chocolate from the brownie still on his teeth. "The best. Where are we off to now, Tubbs?"

"Uh, I'm Crockett, remember? Ice-cream-colored suits, shoes with no socks?"

"Right. I forgot. Must be all the sugar." He licked his fingers for emphasis with a broad grin.

Giggling, I said, "We need to find Millie. She's here tonight. Use all that height of yours to see if you can find her. She's a tiny blip of a woman with pin-curled dark brown hair. Early sixties, if I remember right.

Almost always wears a pair of sweats and a fun sweat-shirt, and don't forget the hearing aid. Probably with her grandchildren."

He paused for a moment, his eyes scanning the crowd. "In the back of the lodge by the hot chocolate fountain. She's with two little white-blonde-haired girls in fancy Christmas dresses."

My eyes zeroed in on the direction Hobbs pointed toward. "Got it. You want in, or is there more dessert to be had?"

"Lemme grab some more of those lacey cookies and I'll be right behind you." He planted a kiss on my nose and went back to the dessert table.

I made my way toward petite Millie, who was busy looking on the shelf of a bookcase for the scavenger hunt.

I didn't know Millie Hart at all other than the few times I'd seen her here at the lodge. Though, I did know she was famous around town for her colorful sweatsuits, which I fully understood when I saw her.

She wore a Christmas-themed sweatsuit with tiny red, white, and green pom-poms sewn to the wrists of the shirt and a big candy cane on the front.

As I approached, I smiled at the two girls in their ruffled Christmas dresses, no more than maybe five and eight. "Hi, guys! Mind if I talk to Grandma for a minute?"

"Girls, go find your mama. She's right over by the fireplace. I'll see you in a minute." As the girls skipped off, Millie turned back to me. "You're that detective lady, right?" she asked with a clearly hesitant smile, touching her ears to adjust her hearing aids.

I held up my hands and shook my head. "Heck no. I'm not a detective. I own Just Claus."

Her expression became instantly lighter. "Aw, sure-sure. I knew your mom, Keeva. I'm a little bit older than she woulda been, but we went to high school together. She was a nice lady. Sorry about your loss."

Hearing someone knew my quirky mother always made me a little sad. They held the key to her memories, some I'm sure she didn't have the chance to share with me, and it never failed to catch me off guard.

"Thank you," I murmured. "I'm Halliday, by the way." I held out my hand and she took it in her calloused palm, giving it a firm shake.

She tucked her fingers over her ear and nodded. "Nice to meet you. What can I do for you, Halliday?"

"I hear Joey Scarpetti talked to you about a room?"

Her expression turned worried and her eyes filled with watery tears. "Oooh, I can't tell you how sorry I was to hear he was killed. Who would do such a thing to such a nice boy?"

I was confused. "But I thought he upset you?"

She flapped her winkled, work-worn hands at me. "Bah! That was nothing. I was frustrated because I couldn't hear him and he was frustrated because he wanted answers. He apologized, and then he came all the way down to the laundry room to apologize again. He was a good boy who just got a little upset. We made up and it was fine."

Sheesh, even the person he'd yelled at thought he was a nice boy. "What did he want to know about the rooms on the first floor?"

"He wanted to know if I'd ever seen anything suspicious going on. If I'd ever seen someone go into one of the rooms up there who didn't belong."

"Suspicious? Do you know what he meant? Did he say? Like, was it about a girlfriend? Wife? Friend?" I knew I was rambling, but this was the most information I'd gotten since I started sticking my nose in where it didn't belong.

But Millie shook her head and bit her lip. "He didn't say what it was about. He just said it was really important. He also didn't say why he wanted to know, but he did say it was vital. That's the word he used. *Vital.*"

"Do you remember when this conversation happened?"

Clarissa said it happened a couple of days ago— which meant if Joey were here at the lodge, looking into something nefarious, he hadn't been wasting time before he talked to Millie.

"It happened just the other day. He asked about a specific room, but I couldn't remember anything weird going on. Nothing suspicious, for sure."

Zing! There went that internal alarm. "Which room was that?"

Then she gasped as though she realized something, wringing her hands. "Aw, no. No, no, no!"

"Millie, what is it?"

But the lurch of my stomach told me I already knew. Millie's answer would only be confirmation.

Her hand went to her face, her expression stricken. "It was the Talbots' room, Halliday. He asked about the Talbots' room!"

CHAPTER 12

"*A*nd they found that camera in there, didn't they? Oh, nooo. What have I done?"

My stomach took that plunge again, but I reached for her hand to soothe her. "Millie, you didn't do anything. I promise you didn't. But you just helped me and probably the police a ton. Please don't fret."

But her gray eyes were frantic and her bottom lip trembled. "He was such a nice boy!"

"He was, Millie, and you've done the right thing by telling me what you know."

"When I heard he'd been…" She stopped and swallowed, her face pale. "When I heard he was dead and that they found a camera hidden in the Talbots' room, I didn't make the connection. If him askin' around is what got him killed… Oh, I just couldn't stand it!"

"It had nothing to do with you, Millie. I promise. He was asking about that specific room for a reason. And you did the right thing by doing your job and preserving the Talbots' privacy."

Millie seemed to accept that, but she gripped my hand anyway. "I'd better tell the police about this, huh?"

Patting her hand, I agreed. "I think that's a great idea. I'll text Officer Fitzsimmons for you. He's a friend of mine."

She gave me a hesitant look, her eyes searching mine. "Do you think he's going to be mad?"

"Absolutely not. How were you to know what would happen? Listen, it's okay. Let me bring you to your daughter, all right?"

Her hand went to her throat is clear dismay. "That poor boy!"

I hooked her arm through mine and led her through the crowd to her daughter, a pretty white-blonde like her daughters, who encompassed her mother in a hug when I explained why she was so upset.

Leaving the two of them together, I caught up with Hobbs who, by some miracle, had found an empty plaid winged-back chair by the back of the lobby where it was a bit quieter.

While people ran from place to place on the scavenger hunt, he patted his knee when he saw me. "Sit, take a load off, and tell me what you found, Crockett."

I sat on his lap and shook my head in frustration. "Not much more than what we mostly already knew. Joey did want to know about the Talbots' room. He wanted to know if Millie saw anyone suspicious go into their room. What I *really* want to know is, if he was asking around and the person who put the webcam in there heard about it, why would they leave it in there?"

"I have no idea. But if nothing else, it's confirmation he asked about that specific room. Something we didn't have before. It explains your uneasy feeling upon entry."

It did explain that. It didn't explain why the webcam was still there. Maybe the killer left and didn't bother to remove it because their job here was done?

Strangely seductive music came from Hobbs's phone, distracting me. He quickly looked around while he turned it down.

"What are you doing?"

"Listen, call me crazy, but for the sake of the investigation…I joined Uncensored Intimacies."

"You did what?" I yelped, then lowered my voice to a whisper when I caught some odd looks. "Why did you do that?"

"Because what if you're right and the woman in your vision is on this site? You might be able to identify her."

I blanched. That was fair. I almost hoped I wouldn't have to, but it was a good idea. "Okay, that makes sense, but aren't all the videos anonymous? It's not like her name's going to be there. Not her real name, anyway, or her address."

"That's true, but maybe we'll see something in the background that'll give us a clue to the killer. Something in the environment around her that could help us find her. Not long ago I watched a documentary about how a bunch of people from all around the world who met up on the Internet caught a serial killer just by putting their heads together and finding clues about the surroundings of the guy. He was arrogant enough to put some of the videos he'd made online and the Internet sleuths helped catch him."

"He made videos of his serial killings?" I was horrified. That was sick.

"Not exactly. It's kind of a long-ish story. Suffice it to say, the Internet sleuths were able to catch him because they researched, of all things, a doorknob."

That gave me a little hope, but then I wondered, "Who's looking at the *environment* in one of those videos?"

He winked, his dark lashes sweeping his cheek. "Me. I'm pretty good at details like that. But first, we have to find her. You'd be surprised what you can find out from a doorknob or a piece of clothing, or a million things no one thinks about. Something else to note, I've read some reviews on this mess of a site...and some of them are revenge porn videos."

Well, toad spit. "From people who can't be prosecuted because it's in Macedonia..."

"Exactly."

Frowning, I fell back into the pool of the helpless. "There must be a zillion videos, Hobbs."

"There are, but they have a search function to put in your...uh, *preferences*."

My cheeks went red and hot. "Oh."

It was all I could manage to say, but I was glad Hobbs had taken on the job of looking through the videos. Though, he'd probably need all night and the clock continued to tick.

Hobbs laughed. "Listen, I'm sort of new at this, too. So don't internalize any crazy theories about me and a site the likes o' this one, Crockett. I'm a gentleman. My mama wouldn't have it any other way. It's just something that came to mind in order to catch a possible killer."

I patted his knee. "I get it. It's a great idea, even if it makes my stomach a little queasy that the woman in my vision might be in a video."

With those words, I stiffened and my heartbeat began to crash in my ears.

"Why are you doing this? Who are you?" someone screamed, the voice filled with raw agony. *"You're ruining my life!"*

The voice was disembodied, female, a sound in an endless sea of black, and then there was movement as the picture became clearer.

The woman again, her burgundy hair covering the side of her face. She was at a desktop computer, crying, sobbing so hard her shoulders quaked. I wanted to reach out, console her, ease her tangible suffering.

Please! Please let me help you! my mind screamed.

But of course, she couldn't hear me and I was rooted to the spot, in this dark place where there was nothing but a woman sitting at a computer, crying hysterically.

As it came even closer into focus, I saw a mug next to the computer. A purple mug that read #1 Teacher. My heart raced, beating under my skin, throbbing as though it would burst if it didn't get out.

A teacher...was she a teacher?

Who are you? What's your name? Please, please talk to me!

Out of the pitch black, a slicing sound echoed in my ears. Whoosh, whoosh, whoosh! Whatever it was, it thwacked the air in quick, sharp stabs.

Then I saw it, a quick glimpse, nothing more. What the heck...*a sword?*

A sword!

It was a sword, weaving in and out of the darkness, swishing, swirling, headed for the burgundy-haired woman's neck. Closer and closer the sharp point gleamed, moving toward her.

Move! Run! Turn around!

At that exact moment, she turned her head, but her face was blocked by the enormous sword. It whizzed straight for her, hurtling in the dark, and then she screamed. Long, piercing, painful, until I thought my eardrums would burst.

"Hal! Hal, honey. It's okay. I'm here."

Hobbs. Hobbs was here. I was with Hobbs.

My heart snapped back to life, lurching me forward, but he had a hold on me, tight around my waist. I was still on his lap, safe in his arms.

Then I heard Saul, his gruff Maine accent drowning

out the residual scream. "Migraine?" I heard him ask with sympathy in his tone.

"Yeah," Hobbs acknowledged. "I've got her, though."

I felt a rough hand caress across my cheek. "Poor kid. Let me know if I can help."

Hobbs ran his hand over my back. "Thanks, Saul."

I forced my eyes open to see Hobbs's worried gaze on me, the activity of the room continuing around us. I attempted a smile to reassure him I was all right…but I wasn't actually sure I was.

"Bad one?"

"Scary. A scary one." I shivered at the memory.

"That's two in one day, honey. Isn't that a lot?"

Every nerve in my body felt raw, as though someone had run sandpaper over all of them. "Sort of. But to me, it means a sense of urgency. It's a message from the universe."

"Wanna talk about what the universe just told you?"

I patted his arm and answered in a hoarse voice, "Yes. Soon, but not now. Or rather, not here."

Hobbs held up his phone, giving me a small smile. "Good news though. Saul sent us the list of people who've stayed in the hotel. You can find it in your email."

"That *is* good news," I whispered.

"Honey. You need a break. No more for tonight, okay? Whatever just happened was bad, and it's taking a toll on you."

I gripped his silly Christmas sweater with the

Grinch on it and shook my head. "I can't stop, Hobbs. That woman's life is at stake. *I can't.*"

His sigh was ragged. "But we don't even know if that hasn't already happened, Hal. I know you want to fix this, but you're exhausted."

Stubbornly, I refused to give in. Rising, I decided to go listen in on some more conversations as I went through the list of guests who'd stayed at the lodge. We'd gotten a little information eavesdropping once, why couldn't I again?

"I'm not giving up, Cowboy. Either you're with me till the end or you can go home and rest. I'm not quitting."

My legs wobbled and my knees felt like soft butter, but by Goddess, I was going to finish this. As I turned to leave, Hobbs grabbed my hand.

"Hold on there, Cowgirl. You're not going anywhere without me when there's a maniac on the loose."

I stopped amid all the cheerful people to look up at him, an eyebrow raised. "Why, because you're the big bad man and I'm the helpless female?"

I was being petty again—that was also twice in one day. Shame on me.

"No. Because if you do something cool with your you-know-what, I wanna see. Now don't be a party pooper. Let's go see what else we can find and look over that list."

I couldn't help but laugh, and it broke the sour mood I was in. "Fine, but fair warning. I can do unspeakable things to your underwear. You'll have a rash you'll never forget."

"Oooh. Revenge spells. I like it."

Rolling my eyes, I gripped his hand to let him know I was over myself as we pushed our way back through the crowd in the lobby.

In a corner of the space beside the entry to the café, I saw Abel and Clarissa. For a split second, Abel looked angry, before he saw us and flipped a switch, turning back on his cheery smile.

As we approached them, I asked, "Everything okay, guys?"

Abel turned his charm all the way up, his lean face beaming. "We're fine. Just a disagreement over some guest activities. Nothing we can't work out."

Clarissa smiled, but her eyes didn't match her expression or the tightening of her jaw. "Everything's fine. I have to get back to the scavenger hunt. Catch you guys later."

She waved over her shoulder, her ponytail bouncing behind her head as she ran off.

"I, regrettably, have to do the same. Honestly, if one more guest complains about not being able to ski when we have a madman on the loose, I'm going to lock them outside and let 'em sleep there," he said on a chuckle. "I'm off. See ya later!"

He followed after Clarissa, who'd disappeared into the crowd of people.

"See? Eternally sunshiney," Hobbs muttered about

Abel. "Did it look like they were arguing or was that just me?"

Wiping my clammy hands on my jeans, I shrugged. "I'm not sure, but Clarissa sure looked uncomfortable."

And I was feeling poorly again.

Not the kind of poor as in flu-like poor. That feeling of dread I'd only been able to shake for a time before it came roaring back in a rush of fear.

That was when I got a text from Stiles.

Joey had a ton of cuts to his skin, aside from the puncture that killed him. Coroner has begun to wonder if the person who did this knows their way around a knife or a sword.

I froze on the spot, my throat going dry. The sword in my vision…

I tried to text him back, but another text came in just as fast.

Think we might have found a real suspect.

My intestines tied themselves in a knot. *Who?* I texted back.

Can't talk now about details, but we found the murder weapon and Marcelle's fingerprints were on it. Will call later. Stay safe, Kitten.

Hobbs looked over my shoulder. "What's going on?"

I held up my phone and showed him the message about Marcelle. "Told ya we should never underestimate the little guys, Texas."

CHAPTER 13

*W*e'd decided to drive back to the house for the time being after getting Stiles's text about Marcelle. If Marcelle was being questioned, maybe this was over.

That didn't sit right with me, but what do I know?

As the lights of town sat in the rearview mirror, Hobbs suddenly said, "It's not him. I'm tellin' you, Cowgirl, he's not our guy."

I gripped the arm of the door because I mostly agreed with him. Yet…

"Then why are his fingerprints all over the murder weapon? And only his fingerprints, by the way."

Hobbs hit the steering wheel with the heel of his hand. "He does work in the ski shop."

"But the ski pole, aka murder weapon, wasn't from the lodge's ski shop," I pointed out.

"There's some kind of explanation, believe that. No way did that kid kill Joey Scarpetti."

I glanced at him over the dashboard lights of his Jeep, his strong jaw set and determined. "Just because you don't think he's strong enough to have dragged Joey back to the lifts?"

But Hobbs shook his head with a firm bounce, his lips thinning. "It's not just that. It's his vibe, I guess. I don't know. I can't explain it, but it's not Marcelle. And that's another thing, who says Joey was dragged back to the lifts? Maybe he ran and whoever killed him, chased him."

"His carotid was nicked, Hobbs Dainty. How's he running anywhere?"

"Maybe it happened *after* he got to the lifts? He was pretty cut up, but that doesn't mean the fatal blow was by the pear tree."

Yep. That made complete sense. Gosh, my boyfriend was smart, wasn't he? "That's why you're Tubbs and I'm Crockett. Crockett was more concerned with how he looked, Tubbs was the smart one. And you're right. I never thought of that."

"And I still don't think Marcelle had anything to do with it."

I tended to agree with him because Marcelle didn't feel right, but why were his fingerprints on the ski pole —one that wasn't the lodge's property?

As we pulled into the driveway, the Christmas decorations couldn't even make me smile. The front porch glowed with twinkling lights, draped over the bannisters and along the eaves.

The two rocking chairs I used to love to sit in with

my grandmother, now with cheerful red and white throw pillows on them, almost always brought a happy memory of summers gone by, sitting and listening to the ocean roar and the seagulls cry, with glasses of lemonade as we whiled away an afternoon.

But tonight? Tonight they left me unmoved, almost bereft, and I couldn't shake it. This particular murder was hitting me harder than most. I didn't know Joey or the woman in my visions, so being as invested as I was probably appeared foolish. But I felt connected to them somehow, and the visions were really doing me in.

"You've got a light out on the front porch."

I looked up in the direction Hobbs pointed, past the blanket of snow and to the eaves of my L-shaped ranch house. "So what else is new. With over fifty-thousand lights, there's always one, isn't there?"

Hobbs chuckled. "I'll fix it. You go inside and warm up. See what the kids are up to."

That warmed me. My happy place was my house filled with our pets and my familiar. "I've got to feed Nana Karen first. You wanna come?"

"Still need a little time, if you don't mind," he mumbled on a cough.

Laughing, I nodded my understanding. "I get it. It's hard enough with Atti, but a reindeer is just crazy, right?"

He grinned. "It might take a minute, I think. But I'll get there."

I gave him a warm smile of understanding. "Okay. See you inside?"

"You bet. I'll have the laptop and some wine ready and waiting."

I leaned over and gave him a kiss. "My knight in shining cowboy hat. See you in a minute."

Hopping out of the car, I headed to the barn to check on Nana. The ocean roared, churning and swirling, a sure signal we were in for some bad weather. The night air was bitter cold and raw, but the lights that led the way to the barn made me feel a bit better.

I pushed the door open to find my nana sound asleep. As quietly as I could, I checked her water and food. She hadn't eaten much since this morning, which meant she'd found candy canes somewhere. It also explained her mid-evening nap. She'd crashed from her sugar rush.

Deep in thought, I went over the day's events, my brain buzzing with activity.

"How goes it, Sugarbuns?"

I jumped, dropping the broom. "You scared me, Nana! Don't do that."

She rose on all fours and hauled her big body upward. "Sorry, honey. So how goes it with my favorite hunk?"

"It's fine, I guess. We're business as usual."

And we were. I was trusting him to explain in his own time who that woman was. I told Nana all about the events of the day, finding out about Leona, and where we stood with our amateurish investigation.

"First, holy cats, Hal! He really fell off the ski lift?

Sheesh, I can't tell you how many times I was afraid of that happening. Never expected it'd be a dead body."

Snorting, I agreed. "Me neither. But it was and it's been madness ever since."

"And how do you feel about my boy telling you he wasn't cheating on you. You believe him?"

I nodded without hesitation. I didn't know what Leona was about or why she had to be there when he told me whatever he was going to tell me, but I believed him. "I do." And as I said the words, I meant them. I *felt* them this time.

"Good, because all I can say is, based on our conversations, no way he's two-timin' ya."

I stroked the top of her head, scratching her antlers. "I trust you and your opinion, and he was very honest with me about Leona."

"Tell ya one thing. Sure am glad my hottie was there to help you through those visions. They were humdingers, huh, Punkin'?"

Sighing, I leaned against the rail post of her stall. "They were awful, and I'm terrified I'm going to be too late, Nana."

She nudged my arm with her muzzle. "Aw, Hallie-Oop, you can't control everything. You know that. The universe has a plan and there's nothing you can do to stop it."

Tears stung my eyes, frustrating me. "But I can try."

Nana nuzzled my arm. "You sure can, and I'm proud of the woman you've become, fighting for good.

But you can't be everywhere, Sugarplum. That's just the truth."

"So I should just give up?" I whimpered, something very unlike me.

"No. That's not what I'm saying at all. What I'm saying is, you have no control over the plan, and you can feel bad about it, you can cry about it, but then you have to let it go with the knowledge it was never in your hands to begin with."

I took a deep breath and wrapped my arms around Nana's neck, pressing my cheek to hers. "You're right. I wish you were still here in Nana form."

"I *am* still here in Nana form. The only thing that's changed are my boobs aren't at my waist anymore and now I have antlers."

I burst out laughing, letting the tears fall down my cold cheeks. "I love you, Nana."

She rubbed my cheek with her cold nose. "Love you back, pretty girl. Now go figure this out with Hot Sauce Hobbs so me and him can have a nice talk about how he should look after my favorite girl."

I gave her one last squeeze. "I will. See you in the morning."

She snorted and settled back on her haunches before lying down in her stall. "You better believe it."

"Sweet dreams," I whispered as I covered her with her favorite blanket and headed back to the house.

Closing the barn door behind me, I tromped through the snow, catching a glimpse of Hobbs in the kitchen, uncorking a bottle of wine. Handsome and tall, he looked comfortable in the space as he moved to grab wine glasses and scoop up Phil, who was a little in love with Hobbs.

He nuzzled him before setting him on the floor and gathering up tiny Barbra to drop on his shoulder as he pulled some cheese and crackers from the fridge. His familiarity made me smile.

My heart fluttered deep in my chest, and in that moment, I knew he was telling me the truth. I truly knew.

I also knew he'd help me figure this out as long as I was willing to try and find out who the woman was.

She'd become even more important to me than discovering who'd killed Joey.

With new determination, I headed back into the house.

A
s Hobbs sipped his wine, he scrolled videos on Uncensored Intimacies, stopping each time he saw someone with unusual-colored hair.

"Anything?" I asked.

"Nope. Not yet. And quite frankly," he said as he turned his head sideways, "I didn't know some of this was possible. Physics don't seem to matter to these people."

I giggled. "Thanks for taking the hit on this on."

"It's the least I can do. Hashtag team HAH," he joked.

Groaning, I rested my head in my hand and blew out a breath of exasperation. "I wish we had more to go on. The only other clue we have is that she *might* be a teacher. Maybe we should be looking up teachers with the name Sabrina? We're never going to find her at this rate, Hobbs. I don't even know what she looks like other than she has burgundy hair."

He grabbed my hand and entwined his fingers with mine. "But you know what the room Joey wanted to see looks like. The logical conclusion to draw is she stayed in that room. If we find a video, maybe we'll find a clue like the Internet sleuths."

If...

I looked at the PDF Hobbs had printed for me—the one Saul had sent to both our emails—of all the people who'd stayed at the lodge over the last two years, which, by the way, was a lot of people.

So many people.

I was only halfway through the list, but so far nothing. Pushing the printout away, I fought a sleepy spell with a long yawn.

"You're beat, honey. I don't want to sound like a broken record, but…"

"Coffee. Coffee will help me. I need a jolt of caffeine."

Hobbs pushed his chair out, the scrape on the hardwood loud in the silence. "I'll make it."

Snapping my fingers, I produced a steaming cup of coffee with cream on the table. "You want one, too?"

He mock-gasped. "Won't Atticus raise a stink if you use your magic for personal gain?"

"Not tonight, he won't," Atticus said as he flew into the room, his colorful wings buzzing. "How are you, Halliday? Can I get you anything?"

I smiled at him, though it exhausted me to lift even my face muscles. "No. Thanks, Atti. I'm fine."

He landed on the table's surface, cocking his head at me as he sauntered across the printed paper. "Where are we in this investigation, Poppet? When can you call it a night?"

I squeezed my temples to ease the ache. "Not until I find out who and where the woman in my vision is. Then I'll stop."

Atti snorted his disapproval. "Precious child, that could be in an hour or it could be next year! You must take a break. You look positively dreadful with those circles under your eyes, which are as red as the ornaments on the tree."

"I'll be fine once I get some coffee in me. Now go to bed." I shooed him off the printout. "It's almost eleven. Way past your bedtime."

But he flapped his wings in indignation. "I'll do no such thing. Let me help you, Poppet. What can I do?"

I fought a burst of tears and instead sipped my coffee. "Can you help me find the name of the woman who wants to take her own life? Maybe she's on that list there. But I mean, who knows, right? We could be all wrong about everything and then she'll die and—"

"Halliday Valentine, stop this right now!" Atti chastised, wobbling his way over to put his tiny beak in my face. "Gather yourself this instant. If I've said it once, I've said it a hundred times. We do not give up. *You* will not give up. I won't let you. Now, have your coffee, for which I won't scold you for producing out of thin air, and pull yourself together. We have a young woman to find and if we don't find her, it won't be because we didn't try!"

There was nothing like an Atticus Finch pep talk to set you back on the straight and narrow. Squaring my shoulders, I heeded his words and looked closer at the list.

That's when I heard Hobbs gasp and push the laptop away.

"Do tell, Mr. Dainty. Have you found some new form of intimacy you weren't aware of that now has you enrapt?"

Hobbs shook his head and sighed with a hangdog grin. "No, sir, but I think I just stumbled on something pretty important." He pushed the laptop toward me and pointed to the tab that read Coffee is Life, the place from the receipt we'd found. He clicked it, and everything began to swirl in front of my eyes.

My mouth fell open. It was the woman with the burgundy hair. Same cut, same color.

And her name?

Sabrina Caldwell.

CHAPTER 14

"*M*otherclucker! I can't believe you found her!" I yelped, suddenly wide awake as I stared at the pretty face of Sabrina Caldwell.

Poor Stephen King groaned at my excitement, stretching his stout body in his bed as Phil snuggled closer to him.

Sabrina did, indeed, have burgundy hair. She was petite with a heart-shaped face, full lips painted red and a wide, generous smile. She stood next to a tall, lean man with round glasses and a thick thatch of brown hair. He had a T-shirt on that read Coffee is Life, worn jeans and an apron.

Hobbs pointed to the screen. "That's her boyfriend, Igor Brown. He owns the coffee shop. And her brother is—ready for this? *Grady* Caldwell." He pointed to the man who looked exactly like Joey.

Happy. Alive. With his sister, who loved the color purple and was a teacher.

I hopped up and ran around the table to kiss him smack on the lips, bracketing his face with my hands. "You're amazing! How did you figure that out?"

"Yelp reviews help a lot more than just finding out how good the coffee is. It was just a chain of events. Someone mentioned how great the coffee was and how much they liked the reno Igor did recently. Then I went to their Facebook page and found pictures of not just the reno, but of Igor's girlfriend *Sabrina* and her brother, Grady, all with him, helping with the renovation, and all tagged in the pictures. I followed the tags to their respective pages, and while they're mostly private, I saw they both live in Westbrook, where the café is. Sabrina's a teacher and Grady's a software engineer."

I gave him another big fat kiss. "You're the smartest person I know."

"Ahem!" Atti cleared his throat in indignation. "Pardon?"

Grinning at him, I stroked his tiny head. "You're smart, too, Atti. Now, we have to pass this on to Stiles. I'd better text him because we have a *whaaat*?"

"A lead!" Hobbs sang out, scaring a sleeping Barbra Streisand, who lifted her gray fuzzy head and gave it a shake in confusion.

"Yes! We have a lead!" I repeated, reaching for my phone in my back pocket. Frowning, I discovered it wasn't there. "Did I leave my phone in your car?"

Hobbs, who was intently looking at the Coffee is

Life Facebook page, shook his head. "I don't know. Want me to go check?"

"Nope, you keep working your magic, and please send Sabrina a message on Facebook. I don't know if she'll get it because we're not friends, and she might find you suspish because you're a cute guy, but at least we can try. And while you do that, I'll check your Jeep."

Grabbing my coat from the back of the chair, I ran out the front door to the driveway, only to be hit in the face with fat snowflakes.

I zipped to the car, my sleepy spell gone, and pulled it open, checking for my phone. I looked under the seat and on the floor, but nothing.

Well, dang.

Running back inside, I remembered the last time I'd used it was when I was texting Stiles at the lodge. I must have left it there. Probably after being so shaken up by my vision.

Hobbs could text Stiles for me, but I had some sensitive stuff on my cell I'd rather people didn't see…

I thought of Hobbs's warning earlier today about putting a passcode on it, and I wanted to kick myself.

"I think I left it at the lodge. Would you call and check?"

"You bet." He scooped his phone up and punched in the number.

"Marshmallow Hollow Ski Lodge, how may I direct your call?" someone on the other end said.

Hobbs handed it to me. "This is Halliday Valentine. Who is this?"

"It's Abel, Miss Valentine. Bet you're calling about your phone. You left it here at the lodge."

My cheeks went hot, praying he hadn't gone through it. "Oh, thank you, Abel. I'll be right over to pick it up." I clicked the phone off and gave it back to Hobbs.

He pushed his chair back and grabbed his keys. "I'll take you, honey."

But I shook my head. "Nope. You keep searching and send Stiles a text with what you found for me, please. I'll be back in a jiff."

Now he held up *my* keys. "Hold up, don't you need your keys?"

Smiling, I shook my head. "Nope."

"Wait, are you gonna…zap yourself there? I thought you said it was a crapshoot and we might end up in Siberia?"

"That's only when I'm under stress. I don't feel seriously stressed right now. I feel hopeful. But I do need to get my phone back before someone goes through it and sees those pics I took this morning. It's quicker— and no guff from you, Atti," I warned.

Hobbs gave me that look he gave me when he was going to remind me he'd told me so. "I told you to put a passcode on it."

"You sure did, and the second it's back in my hands, I will. Now please text Stiles for me and message Sabrina, and maybe even her boyfriend Igor, being very careful not to mention my vision and frighten him until we know better what's going on and if Sabrina's okay."

Hobbs hopped up from his chair as if in protest, but I blew him a kiss and snapped my fingers, not hearing what it was he said.

I landed on the side of the lodge, in an area off the back of the kitchen, where very few people went, and I was grateful that my spell worked just as I'd envisioned in my head.

If nothing else, it meant I was less stressed. I definitely felt better. We'd found Sabrina, and now I needed to get in touch with her and prevent the unthinkable, but we were close—so close—and the relief I felt was enormous.

Looking up at the sky, swollen and heavy with snow, I knew we were in for a big one. Man, it was freezing out here tonight. I tucked my chin into the collar of my jacket and headed toward the lobby doors.

Abel waved to me from behind the door as he scooped up some plastic red cups. He pointed to the front desk with his eternally sunshiney smile. "It's over there on the desk."

"Did you get stuck with cleanup?" I asked, looking around at the cluttered tables and the mussed cushions of the plaid couches by the fireplace.

"Sort of, but I don't mind. I have a bit of insomnia. It helps to work the excess energy off. I'm just doing the rough draft of cleaning. The housekeepers will get the rest in the morning."

Maybe Abel wasn't so bad after all. If nothing else,

he used his time constructively and appeared to be a team player. Still, the conversation he had earlier with Clarissa niggled at me.

"Hey, is everything all right between you and Clarissa? It looked like you two were having an argument earlier."

He gave me a sheepish look, two bright spots appearing on his lean cheeks. "It was really no big deal. We just had a minor disagreement."

He liked Clarissa, that much was clear, but I didn't want to pry into his private life and make him any more uncomfortable. I knew something was bothering him, but I had bigger fish to fry.

"Well, thanks for taking care of my phone, Abel. Appreciate it."

I turned to go grab it when he said, "Miss Valentine?"

"Please, call me Hal."

"Hal. Ever done something because you liked someone, that you later regretted doing?"

I laughed an ironic laugh. If he only knew. "Have I ever. Plenty of times. Why do you ask?"

He looked like he was considering telling me, but then he shook his head and waved me off, but his eyes said he was sad. "It's nothing. I was just wondering. Have a great night, and if I don't see you, have a Merry Christmas."

I reached out and patted his shoulder. "You, too, Abel."

He turned and left, going to the back of the lodge

toward the rear exit, leaving me feeling a little sad for him. It was rather obvious to me that he had a crush on Clarissa, but she'd liked Joey. That could make a working situation very uncomfortable.

Yet, I wondered exactly what he meant when he'd asked if I'd ever done anything for someone I liked that I'd regretted.

Right now, I didn't have time to think overmuch about Abel. I needed to talk to Stiles and we needed to get in touch with this woman Sabrina. I'd never seen her face, but I knew she was the woman in the pictures. I felt it, and that lit a fire under my feet.

I moved quickly toward the front desk to grab my phone when I heard a child's voice say, "Identify yourself!"

Nearly jumping out of my skin, I whipped around to find a little boy of maybe ten or so, in Batman pajamas, holding a shiny, red toy gun. He had a thatch of straight brown hair and mischievous brown eyes fringed with thick lashes.

Once I realized he was playing and my stomach stopped bouncing around, I threw my hands up and smiled at him. "My name is Halliday Valentine. Who, pray tell, is holding me at gunpoint?"

He fought a grin, trying to keep his expression serious. "Carter. Hudson Carter," he said in a pretty good impression of James Bond—accent and all.

"Well, well," I cooed playfully, narrowing my eyes and planting my hands on my hips. "If it isn't the infamous Hudson Carter. What brings you all the way to snowy Maine? Spy convention? Hot on the trail of a jewel thief? Or is someone trying to blow up the world with an atomic bomb?"

He tried like heck to stay in character, but he crumbled into a fit of laughter. "You're funny, and so is your name."

I rolled my eyes with dramatic exaggeration. "Tell me about it. You should have had to grow up with a name like Halliday. So what has you up at this hour, Carter, Hudson Carter, and where's the night manager?"

He grinned, his impishly freckled face turning pink. "He went to the bathroom, but I think that means he went to smoke because that's what he does when it's quiet 'round here."

"And you didn't answer my second question, what has you up this late?"

"Promise not to tell my mom?"

"Well, if you haven't noticed, I'm an adult, and adults are supposed to do the right thing—which would be to tell your mom. But if you promise to go back to bed and stay in your room, I'll lock up my lips and throw away the key."

He shrugged and leaned against the front desk. "I was just playing spy. My mom says you can't grow up and be a spy, but if James Bond can, I don't know why I can't. He was a little boy one time, too."

I scooped up my phone and nodded with a grin. "He absolutely was, and very cool. I love spies."

"Me, too," he said excitedly. "Spies stay up late and

have cool gadgets and they catch people doing things they're not supposed to be doing."

Absently, as I clicked my phone on, I asked, "They sure do. Ever catch someone doing something they're not supposed to be doing?"

"Heck yeah!" he all but shouted. "Just tonight, I caught somebody looking at your phone. They didn't see me because I was hiding over there behind that big fake tree."

I looked to the Ficus in the corner of the lobby, and my spine went rigid. Oh, heavens. This wasn't good. "Do you mean Abel?"

"No. It wasn't a man, it was a girl. I saw her the other night, too. She was following Joey around."

Holy coconuts, this must be the little boy who'd been busting his sister's chops about her boyfriend earlier today, and she'd accused him of creeping around the lodge at night.

My mouth suddenly went dry. "Who was the lady, Hudson?"

"That lady with the ponytail who made up all those stupid games for us today. Can't remember her name."

Clarissa?

Trying to remain calm, I looked around the quiet lodge and decided this was no place for a small child. Who knew who was lurking around here and might hear him.

I was going to blackmail him back to his room, and I didn't even care. "Hudson? Can you do me a favor? If you do, I promise not to tell your mom you were down here so late, playing spy."

"Are you tryin' to bribe me, lady?"

"I sure am. Here's what you have to do if you want me to keep my lips shut. Go back to your room. Go right now and don't come back down until your parents come and get you, okay? If you do, I'll keep my lips zipped." I made the universal sign of a key locking my mouth shut.

Hudson seemed to consider that for a moment, before he nodded. "Okey-doke."

"Where's your room?"

He pointed to the row of rooms at the top of the stairs. "Right there in the middle. I have to share it with my stupid sister, who plays kissy-face with her ugly boyfriend on her phone and cries all night because she's not back at home with him."

Fighting a smile, I ordered, "Scoot now! As fast as you can. I'll watch you go to make sure you're really in your room, okay?"

He blew on the end of his toy gun and tucked it into the waistband of his Batman pajamas. "Yeah. Sure."

"Promise you'll stay in your room till tomorrow?"

"Swear." He held his hand over his heart.

"Then go!"

As he ran up the stairs, I watched until he was in his room before I texted Stiles with what I'd just learned. I didn't know how it all fit, I needed time to process it, but Hudson had just given me a major clue.

When I opened my phone, I'd forgotten I'd left it on

the Facebook app. What Hudson said about Clarissa made me look up her page before I zapped myself back home.

When my eyes fell on her profile picture, I had to fight a gasp out loud.

Because guess what Clarissa's doing in her profile picture?

Fencing.

You know, with a *sword*.

Oh, and she also listed she was in a relationship and it was "complicated."

With guess who?

Igor Brown.

Oh, hellfire.

CHAPTER 15

"I gotta give it to you. You really are like a dog with a bone."

Whirling around, I came face to face with Clarissa, but she was no longer the perky, smiling events coordinator.

Her eyes were hard and glassy behind the muzzle of the gun she held.

Seriously, Universe? Two in a row? Didn't we just do this the other night?

She yanked my phone from my hands and threw it on the ground, stomping on it with her heavy snow boots until it smashed into tiny pieces.

I responded by saying something stupid, because, you know, *stressed*. "Clarissa. What are you doing up this late?"

She sneered a laugh, lifting her chin. "Well, Halliday —or should I call you Columbo? Isn't he a great television detective?"

173

I shrugged. "I dunno. I kinda liked Magnum P.I. He gets forgotten a lot because he was more sex symbol than anything else, but he was also super smart. I mean, there's no denying he was hot because, phew. Hot, like lava hot...but then there's Monk. Not as hot, but definitely as smart, which makes him a little hot, if not hot coupled with some hang-ups—"

"Shut up," she demanded coolly, her eyes scanning my face. "You know why I'm up. And why I have to do what I have to do."

I cocked my head at her as though I had no idea what she meant. "I have no idea what you mean. What do you have to do?"

"Move," she barked, her stare coldull as she held tight to the gun.

"Where?" I squeaked, trying to look around and see if there was anyone with us, but the lobby was quiet.

"Out the back door. Now," she said with an eerie calm that left me chilled to my marrow.

I didn't have a choice, so I walked toward the door —slowly. Very slowly.

But Clarissa came up behind me and jammed the gun between my shoulder blades, leaving a sharp sting behind. "Move," she hissed in my ear.

I went out the door as instructed, my legs stiff as the blast of bitter cold air hit my face. We headed toward the thicket of trees across the way from the lodge, where the ocean met the bit of untouched forest.

Swallowing hard, I forced myself to remain calm. Just a day ago I was almost in the same position, and I'd learned that talking too much confused the perp, and stress confused me, and when I was stressed and confused, I produced dragons.

I wanted to avoid that if at all possible. So I kept my voice even and my eyes on the prize—getting out of this alive. "Why are you doing this, Clarissa?"

"Walk!" she hissed again.

The falling snow spat at my face, pinging my cheeks with wet splats as the sound of the ocean grew closer. "Where are we going?"

"To the edge of the cliff, where you're going to jump to your death," she said quite plainly and far too calmly. "And it's going to be so sad. The local nosy body, beloved by all in the stupid town of Marshmallow Hollow, dead at such a young age. Boo-hoo."

Oh. Well. At least she had a plan, right? It's good to have a plan.

By the way, the edge of the cliff she spoke of? It was a deadly drop with nothing but craggy rocks and freezing cold ocean below. For sure, I was going to die if I didn't try to stop her first.

I guess I could always jump and suspend myself, but of course, that took a moment to figure out a spell, and I think we all know how that works out for me under duress.

I'd be dead on the rocks below in a watery grave, and there'd still be dragons. Or Jason Momoa. He'd shown up once, too.

Or you can be shot, Hal.

That meant I needed to start talking—stir the pot a little.

As we plodded through the almost calf-deep snow, the wind howled harder the closer we came to the water. I hadn't put on a hat or gloves when I'd so smugly zapped myself here, and it was bone-chillingly cold. My lips stuck to my teeth and my eyes burned from the gusting wind.

Which meant I needed to start talking fast. "What happened with Igor, Clarissa?"

She rushed up behind me and shoved me down to my knees, gripping the length of my hair and pressing the gun to my temple. "What do you know about Igor? Don't you dare speak his name!"

Here went nothing.

Gulping, my neck arched backward in her painful grip, I said, "I know that he's Sabrina Caldwell's boyfriend." Then I winced because I didn't even bother to save the biggest bomb for last. Instead, I rushed toward end game.

"*He is not!* He'll never be her boyfriend. He's *my* boyfriend!" she cried, her voice angry and raw as she gripped my hair tighter and shook my head.

That meant I'd touched a nerve. One I decided to rub a little raw.

"That's not what his Facebook page says, Clarissa," I yelled above the howling wind. "It says he loves *Sabrina...*"

She yanked me up so hard, I almost fell backward. "He does not! *He! Does! Not!* He loves *me*—and I told her. I told her she'd never have him! I sent her an email and told her to leave him alone or something bad would happen!"

The skin on my neck was stretched so tight, I thought my flesh might split. "But she does, Clarissa. She has him. Right now in Westbrook at his coffee shop," I taunted, my throat burning and my eyes watering.

Clarissa let out a wail of torment, one I can bet no one would hear because of the roar of the ocean. She threw me to my back in her anguish and put her foot on my chest. I sank into the snow as she ground her heel painfully into my collarbone.

Her eyes, once so friendly and open, were wild with her suffering and her anger that Igor was with Sabrina. "I hate her! She doesn't deserve him! That's why I did what I did! She deserves every minute of the pain she's in after stealing him from me!"

Gripping her ankle with both hands, fighting the cold snow on my back and the violent shivers it produced, I tried to squirm away, but she kept that gun aimed at me.

"What did you do, Clarissa? What did you do to Sabrina?" I spat.

She smiled then, not the smile she'd displayed when we'd first met her, but a smile that was wide and cold and didn't reach her eyes.

"Aw, c'mon, amateur sleuth, you know what I did. I videotaped them when they were here for a lovers' weekend, then put it on a website. That's what you do when dirty-dirty women behave like cheap floozies and need to be taught a lesson!" she said with sick pride, her eyes glassy and gleaming.

Had Igor really been her boyfriend? Call me crazy, but I didn't understand how she could have talked him into coming to the lodge she worked at with his new girlfriend if they'd broken up.

That compelled me to ask, "How did you get them here, Clarissa? Why would Igor come here if he knew you worked here?"

She bent her knees and leaned forward, jamming the gun in my face, her eyes wide and glazed with hatred. "Hah! It was genius, if I do say so myself. I lured them here under the pretense of a lovers' weekend getaway, all expenses paid. When Sabrina called to see if it was real, I assured her it was the gen-u-ine artifact and the rest was simple. I arranged to be gone while they were here and voila! Instant revenge porn! He never even knew I worked here. I sent it to *everyone*, too. Her parents, the parents of her first-grade students, the school she works for—eeeveryone!"

The sick joy she got from that made me want to throw up, but if I hoped to get out of here, I had to listen to her brag.

I blinked the snow from my eyes, falling in fat splotches on my face and soaking my hair. I ask you, why does being held hostage always have to involve me soaking wet?

I fought not to struggle under her foot with that gun staring me down and keep her engaged in conversation while I tried to come up with a spell that would get me the heck out of here.

"But Joey," I murmured, my heart picking up speed, my pulse throbbing in my ears. "Why would you kill her brother? What did he do to you to deserve that?"

Now she narrowed her eyes, shining with victory. "You mean *Grady*? Because he couldn't keep his nose out of it! She went crying to him and he went to the police. But I'm smarter than him, and he couldn't find out where the video had come from. Some software engineer he was, huh? The police wouldn't even help him because they knew Igor belonged with *me*!"

Something was desperately off about her relationship with Igor, but I didn't have time to pursue exactly what that could be.

I tried to arch my neck to relieve the cold seeping into my skin—at this rate, I'd die of hypothermia before she shot me between the eyes. Still, I didn't try to move her foot.

Instead, I asked from frozen, rapidly cracking lips, "Why did he get a job here at the lodge? How did he find out it was you?"

She snorted, her hands shaking, her mouth a thin line of hate. "He was stupid, but he wasn't *that* stupid. When he found out the video was taken here at the lodge, he figured someone who worked here made it. So he applied for a job and played undercover cop because poor Sabrina had to be protected at all costs, and if the cops wouldn't help, he'd do it himself. He

179

made a fake ID with all his tech skills and wormed his way in here and the chase was on!"

Digging my heels into the snow, I began to prepare my escape as I kept her talking. "How did he find out it was you, Clarissa?"

Now Clarissa stiffened, her rage barely contained. "I made a stupid mistake. He caught me looking at Igor's profile on Facebook. I couldn't take any chances. He had to go after that. That part was easy, by the way. A guy who sits at his desk all day does not a worthy opponent make."

"Killing him was easy?" I squeaked.

All those holes in him said he hadn't gone down without a fight. That couldn't have been easy...

Now she pressed the gun to my cheek, her perky ponytail flattened to her head, her jacket soaked in falling snow but her hand steady as a rock. "No, silly! Getting him to meet me so I could explain. I sent him an anonymous text. I told him I had information about his sister and that video. He met me, I caught him off guard...dead nosy body," she said flatly, with next to no emotion and certainly no remorse.

"But how did you get him to the lifts?"

Now she tipped her head back and laughed, her face maniacal, her skin soaked. "He put up a good fight, for sure. He ran, of course, and I followed. It was like he was meant to die on that lift."

Hobbs had been right. He didn't die at the pear tree. He'd died when he got to the lifts.

Is now the time to nitpick, Hal?

That was when a strange fact about the case made me ask, "Why did he take his shirt off?"

"To stop the blood, of course. He bled like a stuck pig!" she crowed, far too animated for me. "But alas, it didn't help, did it? He died anyway. Sad, huh? Bet Sabrina's going to cry so much, Igor'll get sick of her."

Sabrina. Goddess, I needed to get to Sabrina.

I was running out of questions and my legs were going numb when another revelation slapped me in the face and gave me another excuse to keep her engaged. Abel ran marathons...and he regretted doing something for someone...

Why did this always happen when I was in the throes of a death match? Like, I could have used this information before being held at gunpoint?

As snow hit my face and stung my eyes, I let go of her ankle and put my elbows into the snow. "Abel! You talked him into stealing that box Grady had hidden in the ski hut, didn't you?"

She rolled her eyes in disgust. "I sure did, and after he got it for me, that stupid dork whined about it. But he was an easy mark. He likes me, you know," she said with a chuckle. "Men are so pathetic. Like Marcelle. All I needed him to do was touch that ski pole and then I threw it somewhere I knew the police would find it. Easy-peasy-lemon-squeezy!"

Poor Marcelle, who was being questioned right now. He must be terrified. Hobbs was right. He wasn't the killer.

"Does Abel know you were the one who killed Joey...er, Grady?" I asked, my teeth chattering.

"Don't be stupid, Halliday," she ground out between clenched teeth, spittle forming at the corner of her mouth. "He didn't know why I wanted all the evidence Grady collected in his little box. He didn't even know it was Grady's box to begin with. I just told him not to get caught getting it for me. But I did pretend to be interested in him until he got it, then I left him in the wind. That's why he was crying earlier tonight—because he couldn't have his way. Wah-wah."

That explained Abel's question about doing something stupid. Man, she was downright mean.

Which made me ask, "Why didn't you take the webcam from the Talbots' room, Clarissa? Why did you leave it there?"

She tipped her head back and laughed. "You have no idea how lucrative revenge porn is, do you, you knock-off Charlie's Angel? When I saw how much money I was making from Sabrina and Igor's vid, after I took care of Grady, I put it back. Have you *seen* Mr. Talbot? Yum-my! He'll bring in some good hits."

The poor Talbots. This woman was mad—and I was freezing.

Had we covered everything? Was there anything left?

I didn't need to wonder anymore. She hauled me upward by my hair and shoved me forward, jamming that gun between my shoulder blades again.

I winced, sure a bruise was already forming on my

spine, but worse, I was cold—so cold, and it was making it hard to think.

"Clarissa!" I yelled against the wind, digging my heels in as we neared the edge of the cliff. "They'll catch you! I texted Stiles before you stomped my phone and he'll be here any second!"

"You'll be dead and I'll be long gone. No one will ever find me. I've figured it all out, and once I'm settled, Igor will finally realize he loves me and join me!"

Finally realize he loves me? She was bananapants, and I wanted off the Bananapants Express.

But Clarissa gave me a shake before whipping me around and pressing the gun between my eyes.

We were no longer bantering or trading information—her eyes, glittering in the dark, said she was going to kill me and there would be no discussion.

"Jump, Halliday! Do it!" she roared. "Or I'll push you!"

Welp, I had two choices. Jump or be pushed. I wasn't sure which way would best facilitate my idea about how to save myself, but at least she was giving me a choice.

Now, don't get me wrong, as the wind screamed and my fingers had no feeling, I was terrified I was going to fudge this up and die in the process, but I would do it with my head held high.

"Do it!" I screamed in her face. "Push me, you coward!"

Yep. I dared her to push me over the edge.

The shock on Clarissa's face was well worth the lashing I was going to get—one she gave me by raising the pistol and cracking me in the face with it.

I was slow to spring into action, but I grabbed her wrist and gripped it as hard as I could, hoping to wrestle the gun away from her.

"Let me gooo!" she hollered.

I managed to shove her away long enough to move a couple feet back from the edge of the cliff, but no sooner had I done so, she was right back in front of me.

The gun was askew in her fingers, probably as cold as mine, leaving them stiff. She resorted to clocking me in the face again, a hard right jab to my eyeball that knocked me down.

And then she was hovering over me again, gun repositioned and pointed at me. As I crab-walked to back away, I managed to rise to my feet again and bellow, "Do it, Clarissa! Push me! I dare youuu!"

At that point, I think she'd had it.

So she did what I asked.

She ran at me—so fast, so fueled by rage, she didn't even look like Clarissa anymore, and as she howled her anger, she gave me a shove—one so hard, I thought she broke my shoulder.

Of course, this was when I totally blanked and forgot the spell I was going to use.

Honestly, I needed a good Witch Spells 101 class or something.

Because there had to be a better way.

CHAPTER 16

So I'm here to tell you, I'm not sure it's true that your mind goes blank on your way down in a long fall. Because my mind was anything but blank, and as the ragged cliffs and rocky edges flew past me, all I could think was this is gonna hurt like the dickens if I didn't buck up.

And then I thought about that abominable snowman named Bumble. You know the one. The one in *Rudolph the Red-Nosed Reindeer*? You know…big, hairy, lots of teeth, bouncy…toothache as an explanation for why he was so cranky.

I have no idea why a picture of him flashed through my head, or the sound of Yukon Cornelius hollering "wahoooo" when he knocks Bumble out rang in my ears, but there you have it.

It snapped me into action. "Spirits, lift me! Lift me high! Lift me up to the sky!"

And the spirits complied with a roar.

Okay, so there were some technicalities—like the fact that I was now on the shoulders of...of...

I looked down and gasped.

Of a *Bumble*...

Shut up!

We shot back up in the air like a cannonball from a cannon, cutting through the falling snow and raging winds, his paw reaching out for the edge of the cliff, his claws digging into it to get a grip.

Clarissa, still standing at the edge of the cliff, a look of disbelief on her face as the gun fell from her hands, screamed and began to back away as the Bumble (I swear, that's what I conjured) clawed his way over the edge and hopped up on the ground with me on his back.

The only problem? He chased after her. Roaring and snarling, his big feet clapping like thunder against the snow, all while Clarissa screamed to high Heaven. He was so enormous, I saw the lights of the lodge and the tops of the pine trees from his shoulders as I dug my nails in and prayed I didn't slip off.

"Stop!" I yelled, but he was a conjuring. He wasn't real, though the damage he could do was very real, and he had to be stopped.

I clung to him and wracked my brain, trying to remember how to make him disappear. "Be gone with you, oh conjured one—from this Earth, you must run!"

Now, hindsight said I probably should have prefaced that spell with something soft to land on when I made him disappear. But as per usual, I was panicked and stressed and I screwed it up.

Regardless, with him no longer under me, I crashed into Clarissa, flattening her to the ground with a loud grunt.

"Hal!"

I heard my name, but quite frankly, I was whipped. I'd just dropped from the sky. I could barely lift my head, but I managed to roll off an unconscious Clarissa and lie flat on my back, depleted.

Stiles came crashing through the snow, dropping to his knees to scoop me up. "Kitten!"

My first thought was of Sabrina. Had my vision happened or had I succeeded in changing the future? "Sabrina," I muttered. "Is she okay?"

"We got her, Hal, she's fine."

Relief, so bone deep, washed over me. "Thank Goddess."

"Now, what did I tell you about doing things on your own?"

Oh, that was rich. I burst out laughing. "Shut up, Stiles, and get me up off the ground, would ya? I'm freezing. I'll tell you all about it as soon as I warm up."

"What am I gonna do with you?" he joked as he swung me up in his arms and carried me toward the lodge.

"I don't know about me, but did anyone besides Clarissa see the Bumble?"

He looked down at me as the snow slashed at his

face. "Wait. Like Bumble from our favorite Christmas movie *Rudolph*? You didn't…"

I winced. "I kinda did."

Now he threw his head back and laughed. "I wanna hear all about it. Until then, Hobbs'll be here any minute. I thought he was gonna have a chicken if he didn't find you. Good thing that kid called 9-1-1."

As he set me on the ground near an ambulance, where someone waited to check me, I asked, "Kid?"

He tucked his chin into his thick jacket while police cars and sirens sounded. "Yeah. Hudson something. He called 9-1-1 when he saw Clarissa take you into the woods."

My little spy. Huh.

Stiles dropped a kiss on my frozen cheek. "I gotta go make sure the scene is secure, Hal, but someone will come take your statement. I'll see you tomorrow. It's Christmas Eve…and we have some serious celebrating to do."

I blew him a kiss and let the paramedic escort me to the back of the truck, where he threw a heated blanket around my shoulders and handed me some hot liquid in a Styrofoam cup.

"Hal! Hal, are you okay?" Hudson came running toward me, still in his Batman pajamas.

I slipped off the edge of the truck and gave him a huge hug. "Thank you for calling 9-1-1, Carter, Hudson Carter. You're just like a real spy. A real hero. You probably saved my life."

He grinned at me, his freckles going red on his cheeks. "I know your secret."

I leaned back and eyed him. Uh-oh. "My secret?"

"You're magic!"

I made a face. "Am not."

He jabbed the air with a finger. "Are too. I saw you!"

I played dumb as I sipped the worst coffee I'd ever had. "You must be seeing things."

But he was convinced. "Nuh-uh. I saw you make the snowman from *Rudolph* with my own two eyes."

Crud. "Did you now?"

"Uh-huh," he said eagerly, his eyes bright. "Can I have a pony?"

I started to laugh. "You cannot have a pony, sir. What you can have is my undying gratitude and all the candy canes I can find for the rest of your life if you promise to keep my secret."

He clucked his tongue. "That's not a pony."

"How about a candy cane in the shape of a pony? Or better yet, in the shape of James Bond's golden gun—as long as you eat it responsibly, of course."

His eyes went wide. "You can do that?"

I grinned and winked conspiratorially. "Oh, you'd be amazed at what I can do."

"Hudson!" I heard someone yell, then a woman in a red, fuzzy bathrobe with untamed brown hair was running toward us through the falling snow and wrapping him in her arms as tears streamed down her face. "You had me worried to death! What have I told you about leaving your room at night? I don't know what your sister was doing, but she's in big trouble!"

Hudson snuggled against his mother. "It's okay. I did a good thing, Mom. I called 9-1-1 for Halliday."

I smiled at Mrs. Carter through my swelling black eye. "He sure did. He's a real James Bond. And I'm Halliday Valentine—or am I Miss Moneypenny?"

Hudson broke out into a fit of giggles as his mother excused them and pulled him back into the lodge.

"Hal!" I heard Hobbs call out as he ran toward me, his strong legs taking big strides to get to me. He pulled me close and whispered, "Honey? Thank God you're okay!"

I let him fold me into his warm, strong arms, closing my swollen eyes and sighing. I inhaled the scent of his cologne while I let the warmth of his chest seep into my bones.

"I'm okay," I whispered against his chest.

"I tried to stop you from leaving, but you took off in an awful hurry. You did know there was a killer running loose out here, right?"

I chuckled, then winced. "I'm sorry, but I was so excited we were onto something that I wanted to get my phone before someone saw those pictures."

He pressed his cheek against the top of my head. "Did Clarissa see them?"

"Oh, I'm pretty sure she did. But it's okay now. She's in police custody."

He eyeballed my face when he leaned back. "You need to see a doctor, honey."

But I shook my head. "I just have a black eye and some sore ribs, but I'm okay."

He gave a gentle wipe to my face where snow battered me. "Yeah, you got some shiner there, Cowgirl."

"I'm going to answer whatever questions these nice officers have for me and then I want you to take me home, Texas. I need some wine and sympathy. And a bath. A nice hot bath."

Hugging me close before he let me go, he said, "You got it. Though, question?"

"Can I tell you all about Clarissa after we get back to the house and I warm up?"

Gripping my hand, he sat me gently toward his Jeep. "That's not what I want to know."

"What do you wanna know?"

"What's a Bumble? I overheard that kid telling his mom he saw one..."

I laughed so hard, it hurt my bruised ribs, and I kept laughing long after I'd been questioned and we'd gotten into the car to head home.

EPILOGUE

Christmas eve...

I stared at Hobbs and Leona across my dining room table, the Christmas lights from the windows behind us giving their eyes a gleeful gleam. "This is a joke, right? You two are messing with me?"

Hobbs leaned back in his chair with a smile. "Not a joke, Hal. But do you see why I wanted Leona here with me to tell you?"

I fought for a gulp of air. Not because my ribs were a little sore, but because I was breathless from what they'd just told me. "If you guys had told me you were running away together, I'd find that more plausible than..."

"This?" Hobbs asked with a mischievous grin, holding up the book he'd pulled from his jacket, with a hot guy embracing a sexy woman with long flowing hair, the shiny cover glowing under the light of my dining room table.

"The typewriter!" I all but yelped, scaring poor Phil, who'd been curled up with Barbra and Stephen King by the fire.

That had to be why it kept recurring in my visions. The universe was all but screaming at me the answer, and I'd missed it.

Then I remembered what he'd said...*butt in chair*. Now I remembered why that struck a chord with me. I'd once seen a writer on a Facebook page say, "butt in chair, hands on keyboard."

I shook my finger at my handsome boyfriend. "Butt in chair…"

"What?" Leona asked, her beautiful face confused. "He doesn't use a typewriter. He uses a computer and Word."

I shook my head, forgetting Leona knew nothing about my visions. "Sorry. It's nothing." Then I looked at a sheepish Hobbs, who knew exactly what I meant. "I don't know what to say. You're Savannah Temple? *You?* You write paranormal romance novels? You, a big, strapping Texan? No wonder there are no pictures of you…er, Savannah on social media!"

He reached for my fingers and entwined them with his. "Nope. No pictures—and believe me, there's been loads of speculation about that, which is what I meant about Twitter and a witch hunt. I have a publicist who very artfully dodges all the questions about my gender. And excuse me, but big, strapping Texans can be romantic."

Tucking my hair behind my ear, I shook my head.

"That's not what I mean and you know it. I mean, you're really in touch with your feminine side, aren't you? You write books under a female pseudonym."

"Books you don't like," he very kindly reminded me.

My face flamed hot. "But…but Stiles loves you!" I redirected.

"You don't like Digby's books?" Leona asked with obvious disbelief.

Oooo, I was in hot, hot water. "I didn't say I don't like them. I just said—"

Hobbs clucked his tongue and mimicked my voice. "As I recall, you said to Stiles, and I'm not even paraphrasing here, 'Blick. She's so dark and gloomy and everything is about how awful life is and how hard it is to merely breathe.'"

I winced and bit the end of my nail. Oh, yeah. I had said that. "I just meant I like a funnier take on my paranormal romance, but what do I know? Obviously, people love your dark romances and they clearly don't care if you're a man or a woman or a zebra. You've hit *The New York Times'* Best Seller List a bunch of times. That's proof I don't know what the heck I'm talking about. But it does explain why you knew what a were-deer was."

He gave me a lopsided grin. "It's all good, honey. I get bad reviews all the time. You should see some of my one-star reviews on Amazon. Phew, people can be vicious. But my skin is thick. I mean, it would be nice if my girl liked what I do for a living, but it's nothing I can't live with."

1. Wanted. To. Die. Slide right under the table and D-I-E die.

And I didn't know what to say. So I said something stupid. "I would never give you a one-star review on Amazon or anywhere."

"Well, maybe not now that you know your boyfriend is Savannah Temple," he teased.

Leona clapped her hands on the table. "All right, you two. It looks like you can take it from here, Dig. I'm outta here. I have a hot toddy and a hot girlfriend waiting for me back at the lodge, where I plan to snuggle up under a thick comforter with her in that hotel's big feather bed, watch silly Christmas movies, and be happy to be alive while I stuff my face with those amazing marshmallows from that cute Gracie Good."

She stuck her hand out to me, her long, graceful fingers wrapping around mine. "Hal, thanks for lunch. Best chowder I've ever had, and it was awesome to meet you. You're as gorgeous as Digby said, and I think you're one brave cookie. You're the real romance novel heroine here, lady."

She pulled me into a hug, and I inhaled the scent of her expensive perfume and sighed, only hoping I could ever be as elegant.

"It was really nice to meet you, too, Leona. Thanks for being so nice about how rude I was back at the lodge coffee shop."

She dismissed me with a fine-boned hand. "Bah! No

worries. Digby should have told you long ago what he does so late at night. He brought that on himself. And now, I'm really out. Merry Christmas, darlings!"

Leona left in a cloud of perfume and flawlessness, leaving both Hobbs and I alone to stare at each other until we both broke into grins.

"You're Savannah Temple. Stiles is going to lose his mind."

"And you're a witch," he teased. "We both had secrets."

"What made you decide to write romance novels?" I was dying to know.

"I did it on a bet in college when I teased one of my girlfriends about reading them, and said that anyone could write one, even me. She dared me to try. So I did, and it was awful. Then I got the bug and started reading them one after the other, and tried again. It took a while, but I got an agent—who you now know is Leona—and we sold it to a publisher, and here I am. Still pulling my foot out of my mouth all these years later."

"I'm sorry I said that about your books. But they're so dark and gloomy, and you're so funny in real life. How did that happen?"

He shrugged, lifting his wide shoulders with a grin. "It's what was hot at the time, but maybe now I'll inject a little humor in them. I'm thinking about writing a series with witches. You wanna consult?"

I sipped my mug of hot coffee. "Oh, you bet I do. Boy, can I teach you some stuff."

"I'm counting on it."

"Wait," I whispered as another revelation hit me. "Does Nana know?"

"About my writing? She sure does. She was my biggest brainstormer. I'd talk out a snag in a plot with her and she'd listen."

I couldn't help but laugh. "Dang, can that woman keep a secret."

Hobbs tapped the table with his finger. "Now, back to the issue at hand. What did Stiles say when he called?"

Sighing, I looked down at the table. "Well, Sabrina is alive, but she'd been having some very dark thoughts when she didn't hear from Grady—which confirms, at least to me, the vision of her planning to take matters into her own hands. Of course, she's broken up about her brother, but Igor is with her and they're getting her professional help."

His face went somber. "Thank God. What about Igor and his thing with Clarissa?"

That was weirder than I'd imagined, but I knew something was off about Clarissa and her alleged relationship with the man. "That's where it gets interesting —he doesn't even know who she is. He's never even met her. He was in a Facebook group that she was also in. She'd created this whole fantasy world that revolved around him. She'd been stalking him and making up stories to her mother about her new boyfriend. But the speculation is, when Igor met Sabrina not long ago, Clarissa lost touch with reality."

Hobbs shook his head. "So she never had a relationship with him? Ever? Nothing?"

Playing with the paper napkin, I blew out a breath. "Nope. Nothing. As for Grady, he couldn't get the police to help him, and he couldn't find the user who'd uploaded the video...so he did his own investigative work—undercover, so to speak. He was a good brother just trying to protect his sister."

I was so glad we'd gotten to Sabrina before anything worse happened, but it was still sad. Grady had gone to extremes to help his sister when no one else would, and he'd paid with his life.

"So him catching Clarissa scouring Igor's Facebook page was all just luck?"

"Yep, and it was what tipped him off. Clarissa knew he was suspicious and she took the rest from there."

"Man..." Hobbs said on a sigh. "What about that box Abel got for Clarissa from the ski hut?"

Poor Abel. He'd been duped by Clarissa's feminine wiles. "It had some pictures of Grady's family, of course the ornament for Sabrina and his real identification. A passport and his driver's license."

Hobbs shook his dark head. "That poor guy. Sounds like he was just a decent human being, trying to be a good brother."

"He sure was. But oh! Some good news. They got Clarissa to pull the video of Sabrina and Igor, and she never got to upload the Talbots. Hopefully, that will go a long way toward Sabrina's humiliation in front of her peers."

"That's good news. I'm really glad Sabrina's okay, or will be with some help," Hobbs said, pushing his chair away from the table and taking my hand.

"Me too." *Me too.*

"Life with you sure is an adventure."

I grinned as he helped me up, trying not to wince at my sore ribs. "Said the romance novel writer."

"So, are there any other secrets you have to tell me, Crockett?"

"Not a one, Tubbs. Well, except for my sister Stevie and her fiancé Win—the ex-spy. If you think *my* story's crazy, just you wait," I warned.

He chuckled and dropped a kiss on my lips. "I can't wait. Now, you sit and I'll begin the Christmas Eve festivities. Stiles'll be here in a little bit, so I'd better get on it."

"You're gonna cook a whole dinner when I can just snap my fingers and make it appear?"

"Halliday!" Atticus called from my bedroom. "I heard that!"

Hobbs looked at me and snickered. "I'll get the turkey from the fridge."

I playfully poked him in the chest. "Hey, whose side are you on?"

"Yours. *Always*. Unless Atti's involved. Then I'm out because I'm afraid of him."

"Listen to your beau! He's no one's fool!" Atti called out.

"See? Even Atticus says I'm no one's fool. Except when it comes to you. I'm a little nuts about you."

Snorting, I rested my cheek on his broad chest and sighed happily, even though my eye throbbed and my nose felt like a freight train had run into it. "I'm a little nuts about you, too, Digby Dainty. Just a little bit."

"Merry Christmas, Lacey."

I smiled and snuggled closer. "Merry Christmas, Cagney with the good hair."

The End

Thank you so much for grabbing a copy of *Carnage in a Pear Tree* and going on Hal and Hobbs's latest adventure! I hope this holiday season brings you nothing but peace, joy, and the love of family and friends!

NOTE FROM DAKOTA CASSIDY

I do hope you enjoyed this book, I'd so appreciate it if you'd help others enjoy it too.

Recommend it. Please help other readers find this book by recommending it.

Review it. Please tell other readers why you liked this book by reviewing it at online retailers or your blog. Reader reviews help my books continue to be valued by distributors/resellers. I adore each and every reader who takes the time to write one!

If you love the book or leave a review, thank you. Your support means more than you'll ever know! Thank you!

ABOUT THE AUTHOR

Dakota Cassidy is a USA Today bestselling author with over eighty books. She writes laugh-out-loud cozy mysteries, romantic comedy, grab-some-ice erotic romance, hot and sexy alpha males, paranormal shifters, contemporary kick-ass women, and more.

Dakota lives in the gorgeous state of Oregon with her real-life hero and her dogs, and she loves hearing from readers!

Visit Dakota's website at http://www. dakotacassidy.com for more information.

A Lemon Layne Mystery, a Contemporary Cozy Mystery Series

1. Prawn of the Dead
2. Play That Funky Music White Koi

Witchless In Seattle Mysteries, a Paranormal Cozy Mystery series

1. Witch Slapped
2. Quit Your Witchin'
3. Dewitched
4. The Old Witcheroo
5. How the Witch Stole Christmas
6. Ain't Love a Witch
7. Good Witch Hunting
8. Witch Way Did He Go?
9. Witches Get Stitches

10. Witch it Real Good
11. Witch Perfect
12. Gettin' Witched
13. Where There's a With, There's a Way

Marshmallow Hollow Cozy Christmas Mysteries

1. Jingle All the Slay
2. Have Yourself a Merry Little Witness
3. One Corpse Open Slay
4. Carnage in a Pear Tree

Nun of Your Business Mysteries, a Paranormal Cozy Mystery series

1. Then There Were Nun
2. Hit and Nun
3. House of the Rising Nun
4. The Smoking Nun
5. What a Nunderful World

Wolf Mates, a Paranormal Romantic Comedy series

1. An American Werewolf In Hoboken
2. What's New, Pussycat?
3. Gotta Have Faith
4. Moves Like Jagger
5. Bad Case of Loving You

A Paris, Texas Romance, a Paranormal Romantic Comedy series

1. Witched At Birth
2. What Not to Were
3. Witch Is the New Black
4. White Witchmas

Non-Series

Whose Bride Is She Anyway?

Polanski Brothers: Home of Eternal Rest
Sexy Lips 66
***Accidentally Paranormal*, a Paranormal Romantic Comedy series**

Interview With an Accidental—a free introductory guide to the girls of the Accidentals!

1. The Accidental Werewolf
2. Accidentally Dead
3. The Accidental Human
4. Accidentally Demonic
5. Accidentally Catty
6. Accidentally Dead, Again
7. The Accidental Genie
8. The Accidental Werewolf 2: Something About Harry
9. The Accidental Dragon
10. Accidentally Aphrodite
11. Accidentally Ever After
12. Bearly Accidental
13. How Nina Got Her Fang Back
14. The Accidental Familiar
15. Then Came Wanda
16. The Accidental Mermaid
17. Marty's Horrible, Terrible Very Bad Day
18. The Accidental Unicorn
19. The Accidental Troll
20. Accidentally Divine

***The Plum Orchard*, a Contemporary Romantic Comedy series**

1. Talk This Way

2. Talk Dirty to Me

3. Something to Talk About

4. Talking After Midnight

The Ex-Trophy Wives, a Contemporary Romantic Comedy series

1. You Dropped a Blonde On Me

2. Burning Down the Spouse

3. Waltz This Way

Fangs of Anarchy, a Paranormal Urban Fantasy series

1. Forbidden Alpha

2. Outlaw Alpha

Made in the USA
Middletown, DE
19 September 2023